MHP

FIRST
S H O T

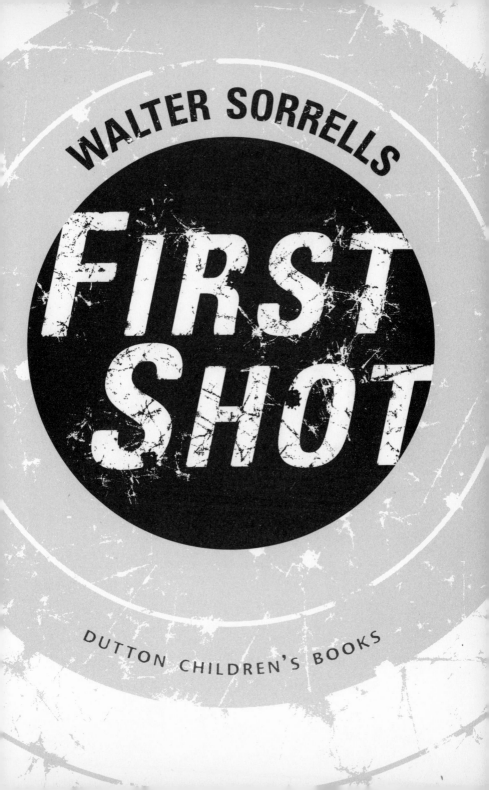

WALTER SORRELLS

FIRST SHOT

DUTTON CHILDREN'S BOOKS

DUTTON BOOKS
A member of Penguin Group (USA) Inc.

Published by the Penguin Group
Penguin Group (USA) Inc., 375 Hudson Street, New York, New York 10014, U.S.A. • Penguin Group (Canada), 10 Alcorn Avenue, Toronto, Ontario, Canada M4V 3B2 (a division ofPearson Penguin Canada Inc.) • Penguin Books Ltd, 80 Strand, London WC2R 0RL, England • Penguin Ireland, 25 St Stephen's Green, Dublin 2, Ireland (a division of Penguin Books Ltd) • Penguin Group (Australia), 250 Camberwell Road, Camberwell, Victoria 3124, Australia (a division of Pearson Australia Group Pty Ltd) • Penguin Books India Pvt Ltd, 11 Community Centre, Panchsheel Park, New Delhi - 110 017, India • Penguin Group (NZ), 67 Apollo Drive, Rosedale, North Shore 0745, Auckland, New Zealand (a division of Pearson New Zealand Ltd) • Penguin Books (South Africa) (Pty) Ltd, 24 Sturdee Avenue, Rosebank, Johannesburg 2196, South Africa • Penguin Books Ltd, Registered Offices: 80 Strand, London WC2R 0RL, England

CIP Data is available.

Published in the United States by Dutton Books,
a member of Penguin Group (USA) Inc.
345 Hudson Street, New York, New York 10014
www.penguin.com/youngreaders

Designed by Jason Henry

Printed in USA ∗ First American Edition
ISBN: 978-0-525-47801-0
1 3 5 7 9 10 2 6 4 2

*To Walker Harris,
my coolest fan*

FIRST
SHOT

WHAT'S WRONG WITH MY LIFE

1. *I am an appendix.*

You know how in biology class they tell you about your appendix? It's like this little worm-shaped thingy hanging off your intestines? And once—a long, long, long time ago—it was useful to our caveman ancestors? But now it's just hanging there, waiting to get infected and burst so you have to go to the hospital?

That's pretty much me.

Vestigial is the fancy word for an appendix. It means: leftover, useless, no longer of any importance.

My name is David Crandall. I go to this private school called The Arsenal. It's in Maine, right on this rocky spit of land sticking out into the Atlantic Ocean. There are paintings of like eight of my ancestors hanging in the halls of the school. They are gloomy, tough-looking characters who all have some important title attached to their name. Senator,

Captain, General, Bishop, Doctor, blah-blah-blah. I don't think I'll ever have some big title like that. I'll just be David Crandall, the appendix. The last useless pointless trivial vestige of the Great Crandalls.

2. *Push-ups.*

The motto of The Arsenal is *Rigor et Disciplina.*

Which is Latin for "push-ups."

There are no fat kids at The Arsenal. Seriously. Not one.

Everybody runs to class. Last kid through the door does push-ups. You want to be in the chess club? You *run* to the chess club. Last guy to chess club does push-ups. You want to write for the newspaper? You run. You want to play soccer? Forget about it! Hungry? Run to dinner. And if you're the last kid? No supper for you, pal. That's policy at The Arsenal. Last kid goes hungry. That's the first thing they tell you when you interview with Colonel Taylor in admissions: You want Junior to eat big piles of yummy food in the comfortable and elegant dining facility? Go elsewhere. Let Junior go eat Cheetos and play video games with all the soft little wusses at Phillips Exeter Academy. The official brochure for The Arsenal describes the dining hall as "drafty and cheerless."

The *official* brochure, dude! Drafty and cheerless!

Would I kid you?

See, the point is that at The Arsenal, everything's a competition. The Arsenal is designed to produce competitors, hard-asses, winners. Winners get hot showers, more food, warmer blankets. Losers get misery. Losers get the crap end of the stick.

And you want to know the worst thing about The Arsenal? My old man's the headmaster, the chief honcho, the guy that ladles out all the *disciplina* and all the *rigor*. Which translates to even more laps and even more push-ups and even more homework assignments and even less food and even colder showers for yours truly.

Because in my father's eyes, nothing I ever do is good enough.

Welcome to The Arsenal. Welcome to my world.

3. *I am invisible to girls.*

I will say this—The Arsenal has a lot of babelicious girls.

But does this do me any good? No. Zero. I'm not the worst-looking guy or anything. But there seems to be something the babelicious girls are looking for that I don't have. I'm not a soccer star; I have no shot at being the best student in the school; I don't have an assload of smarmy charm like Garrett Rothenberg. Basically? I'm not a winner. I'm not a first-guy-through-the-door type of kid.

In fact the only thing I can do well is shoot.

Like, with a gun. Seriously, I'm not joking. I can totally shoot like mad. In fact, up until this year I was the best shooter in the school. Not by a little. By a long shot. (No pun intended.) Which, at most schools, would be like being captain of the chess club. You know, like so what? But at The Arsenal, it's kind of a big deal. For reasons I'll explain.

But now even that's about to change for the worse. I heard rumors there's a new kid at school this year who shoots like crazy. But I'm not worried. I'm the best.

4. *I think my dad murdered my mom.*

But more on that later.

2

Hey, Worm."

It was my roommate, Garrett Rothenberg, talking to me. At The Arsenal no one is called by their first name. You either go by your last name or by a nickname. I've been Worm as long as I can remember. It's not even really insulting anymore.

"What?" I said.

"They posted the results for Dartington Rifles."

"Yeah?"

"You made alternate."

I stared at him. *"What!"*

"Seriously."

"Bull," I said.

"Hey, kiss it, Worm. I'm just saying."

Rothenberg sauntered off, his hands jammed down in the pockets of his khaki pants, his necktie pulled down the perfect amount. There's an art to wearing a necktie. Pull your tie down too far, it's push-ups for slovenly deportment. Leave the knot pulled too tight, you look like a fussy little chump. Like everything else he did, Rothenberg did it perfectly—cool yet not quite slovenly.

I hurried to Crandall House, the administration building. A group of kids was crowded around the bulletin board. I could feel my heart beating. I was the best shooter in the school. Alternate? That was impossible!

Dartington Rifles was the biggest honor in the school. It was part of the Grand Traditions of The Arsenal (a subject my dad can talk about until you about puke). The rifle team doesn't really have anything to do with guns anymore. Not really. I mean, they go out and practice shooting, just like the football team does. But it's only once a week. Mainly Dartington Rifles is just an honor. At the beginning of senior year, the best athletes, the best students, the best citizens, all the first-through-the-door-so-they-never-have-to-do-push-ups crowd gets chosen to be on Dartington Rifles. Oh, plus, there's an actual shooting competition. The final position on the Dartington Rifles goes to the best shooter in the school.

Which was me. The one vestige of the Greatness of the Great Crandalls that still ran in my veins. In addition to being sea captains and Very Reverend Doctors and Secretaries of the Treasury, the Great Crandalls have always been freakin' great shooters.

I shouldered my way through the crowd of kids.

There was the list, written in my father's handwriting

on thick, creamy stationery with the seal of The Arsenal at the top.

Rothenberg, G.

Judge, M.

Willets, A.

Cunningham, F.

Burke, L. R.

Burke, L. W.

Davis, A.

Roloefs, P.

Anand, P.

Cleary, M.

Alternate—Crandall, D.

I stared. Then my cheeks got hot. This was cut-and-dried—best shooter makes the team, a Grand Tradition of the Freakin' School. And I was being robbed!

I pushed through the crowd again, up the stairs, and into the office of the headmaster.

"Hello, Mr. Crandall," Mrs. Erdman said, smiling. All the teachers and administrators call students *Mister*. "Congratulations on Dartington Rifles. Making alternate? That's just *super*."

Super. Yeah, right. "Is Dad in there?" I said.

Her smile faded. "The headmaster is having a conference

with somebody." It was totally verboten for me to refer to him as anything other than *the headmaster.*

I walked past her.

"Mr. Crandall! David! You can't go in there. He's—"

I pushed through the door and into my dad's huge, dim, wood-paneled office. It looked like the office of a president of some big bank back in like 1850. Dad was sitting there with some guy in a really expensive-looking suit. They were laughing about something. There was a certain crinkly thing around Dad's eyes that he always did when he laughed at something he didn't think was funny, but that he thought he'd better laugh at because whoever was cracking the joke was probably about to give a bunch of money to the school. You wouldn't think that would be a whole separate expression for a person to have. But when you're headmaster of a private school that's always short on cash, well, it's a pretty standard thing.

As soon as he saw me, Dad's smile faded.

"Excuse me, Mr. Crandall," he said to me. Dad hasn't called me "David" in years. At least not during the school year. "What do you think you're doing barging in here like that?"

"Alternate?" I said. "Do you have to ruin *everything,* Dad? Am I that big a disappointment to you?"

"Mr. Crandall," Dad said, "you'll refer to me as headmaster."

"Screw that, Dad! For all these years, I've done every single push-up you asked me to, taken all your cold showers, skipped all those meals you took away from me, taken all your crap. And I've never complained. But this isn't *fair*! You know I'm the best shooter in the school."

Dad smiled at the man in the expensive suit. "This is a little embarrassing, John," he said, "but I need to sort out a minor family matter. If you could give me about thirty seconds . . ."

"Say no more," the man said, giving Dad the sort of big fake smile that a rich guy would give to the Mexican dude who cuts his grass, right before he fires his ass for taking a ten-minute break instead of a five-minute break. I recognized the man then. He was the chairman of the board of directors of The Arsenal, a position that always went to some incredibly rich guy who could be guaranteed to give lots of money to the school. He was also my roommate's dad. Yeah, I didn't mention it—but besides being cool and suave and smart and a winner and all that stuff, Garrett Rothenberg was loaded.

Dad's smile went away the minute Mr. Rothenberg left the room. "What in the *world* has gotten into you? John Rothenberg was discussing a major *major* gift to the school. Are trying to—"

"Alternate! I saw the list. You put me down as *alternate*. You know I'm the best shot at this school. I shot eight tens, a nine, and a seven at the Dartington Rifles shooting competition. I bet there wasn't a single kid at this school who shot anywhere close to that."

Dad stared at me for a long time.

"Dad, you can screw me out of a lot of stuff. But not this!" I waved my finger in his face. "Not this!"

He kept looking at me with his the-Great-Crandalls-are-terribly-terribly-disappointed-in-you face.

Finally he turned around and unlocked the ancient mahogany credenza behind him. Then he pulled out a stack of rifle targets and handed one of them to me. I looked at it in disbelief. The center was totally chewed out. Ten tens. I counted, just to be sure. Once, twice, a third time. Ten shots. Ten X rings.

I looked at the top of the target to see who had done this magical shooting. The name was: CLEARY, M.

"This is a joke, right?" I said. "Cleary? I've never even heard of this kid."

"A new student. She's a senior transfer."

"She!" The idea that I'd been beaten sucked bad enough. But . . . by a *girl*? No way. "This is bull and you know it," I said, throwing the target down on Dad's huge old mahogany desk. "Nobody shoots like that. She cheated somehow."

"Mr. Crandall, Miss Cleary happens to be one of the top-ranked female target shooters in the country."

I stared at him. "You mean like a real target shooter? That goes to shooting competitions and stuff?"

He nodded.

"Nobody does that!" I said.

"Apparently they do in Mississippi. She beat you fair and square."

I felt the air slowly bleed out of my lungs. I slumped down in the leather chair. "This isn't fair," I said. "That's cheating or something."

"No, Mr. Crandall, that's competition," Dad said. "She won. You didn't. At The Arsenal, winning is rewarded. Our motto is—"

"Jesus! Dad! I know what the goddamn motto is!"

Dad sat silently, his hands folded across his chest, just looking at me, judging me.

"You can't take this away from me." I felt my eyes narrowing to slits.

"You know the rules. The alternates practice with the team. If a member of the team is removed or has to leave school, the alternate becomes a full member of the team. Only full team members can compete for First Shot."

I wanted to scream. How many times had I heard this? I knew what was coming.

"In its storied two-hundred-and-seven-year history, a Crandall has been awarded First Shot nearly a dozen times. Your great-grandfather was awarded First Shot. Your grandfather was awarded First Shot. *I* was awarded First Shot. It is my job to lead this institution with strict impartiality. I cannot and will not play favorites with you." Dad leaned forward. "But honestly? On a personal level, I would be terribly disappointed if you failed to live up to the record of the great Crandall family."

"Yeah, *right*," I said. There was nothing the guy loved more than watching me fail. Before Mom had died, it hadn't been so bad. But since then? Pure hell.

His voice softened and his headmaster mask seemed to disappear for a moment. I mean, for about half a second he actually looked like the guy who had been my father before Mom died. "Maybe somebody on the team will drop out. You still have a chance."

I shook my head, disgusted. Nobody would drop out. That was a pipe dream. I was finished, sunk, hosed.

"Mr. Crandall," Dad said, leaning back in his chair and putting his headmaster face back on, "this discussion is concluded. After you exit the room, please perform one hundred push-ups for interrupting me during my meeting with Mr. Rothenberg. Then tonight you'll miss Main Meal for insubordination. No, make it tomorrow, since that's roast beef night. Also, for cursing, you'll be on cold showers for the rest of the week."

"Screw that!" I said.

"Make it the rest of the month," he said calmly. "I'll inform Dean Hanley."

I got up, walked to the door, and opened it. The guy Dad had been talking to—Garrett Rothenberg's old man—was blabbing on a cell phone next to Mrs. Erdman's desk, talking in a voice like he was saying something real important and earthshaking, something that the person on the other end was way too dumb and insignificant to understand. He looked at me with cold, indifferent eyes. Like I was nothing but a worm.

I pointed my finger at Dad. "I know what you did," I said.

He frowned. "Excuse me?"

"The other night."

His face went white.

Bam! I thought. *Bull's-eye!*

I walked out. And then I started to panic.

3

First Shot.

I mean, come on, it's the most BS thing in the world. At commencement every year, one kid walks up onstage after all the speeches, and after all the diplomas are handed out he stands in the middle of the stage and loads an old-fashioned, black-powder rifle—pouring in the powder, ramming in the shot, putting the percussion cap on the nipple—ha-ha, lots of jokes about *that*—and cocking the hammer. Then he aims at a target on the far end of Guthrie Field. And shoots.

Supposedly, in like two hundred years, no one has missed.

That shot symbolizes the end of childhood, the acceptance of adult responsibility, the beginning of a life of Achievement and Betterment and Service to Mankind and all the rest of that capital-letter kind of junk.

Like I said earlier, each year the nine top kids in the school—athletes, chemistry geniuses, class presidents, and assorted other Winners and Achievers and guys who don't get stuck doing push-ups all the time—are named to the Dartington Rifles. The tenth kid gets there by winning a shooting competition. The runner-up in that competition is made alternate.

For the entire year, the Dartington Rifles go out on the edge of the Barrens and practice shooting.

Then at the end of the year there's a second shoot-out between the ten members of the Dartington Rifles. The best shooter is named First Shot.

The interesting thing—I mean, at least supposedly it's interesting—is that the guy who places into Dartington Rifles by being the best shooter in the school never becomes First Shot. Never. Well, not since 1861, anyway. Why? Because the other nine Winners and Hustlers and Achievers work their brains out all year and overtake the kid who happens to be a natural crack shot. This is supposed to be a big lesson in life, the kind of thing that The Arsenal is famous for. Sweat trumps talent, blah-blah-blah.

I've been at The Arsenal for six years. I've never been all that great a student. I've never been the first guy picked in sports. I've never been Mr. Popular Student Council Dude. I've never been a babe magnet. I've never been the go-to guy for anything at all. In fact, I'm slightly a loser. Not like a huge loser. Not a Stewy Grainger thick-glasses-and-stuttering-and-failing-gym loser. But kinda below average.

So there's only been one thing I've counted on. And that's winning First Shot. I mean, I have a natural gift for shooting. But on top of that, I've actually practiced. I've actually gone out, year after year, with this clunky old black-powder rifle and shot the stupid thing. Everybody at The Arsenal has to take this class called gunnery. It's another one of the Grand Traditions of the school. But most kids don't take it seriously. Neither does the staff. You come out at the beginning of the year, get a big lesson in firearm safety, goof around with a moldy old rifle, shoot a few rounds, go back to your room. End of story.

But not end of story for me. Like I say, I practiced. I *worked*. All because I was determined to be First Shot. Not just because I'm the appendix of the Great Crandalls. Not just because of my dad and my grandfather and all that crap.

No, it was because of Elliot Crandall III. Elliot Crandall III was the last guy to place onto Dartington Rifles by competition who actually became First Shot. He was supposedly a terrible student, a big disgrace to the the Great Crandall family. But then he went out and won First Shot. He shot ten tens, a feat that has never been equaled since.

The next year he became a first lieutenant in the Union Army. By 1865, he was a brigadier general—the youngest in the entire Union Army. It would have been a great success story . . . except that he got shot in the head at some crummy little battle about a week before the end of the war.

Hence, the shooter's curse.

I had decided way back in seventh grade that I was going to break the shooter's curse. It was totally obvious I'd never be president of the class or win the Chemistry Prize or be captain of the lacrosse team. So I decided I'd break the curse. That would be the one mark I would leave at The Arsenal.

By freshman year there was nobody to touch me. Only Mr. Perfect, Garrett Rothenberg, could give me even a little competition. And he never beat me. Not once.

It was my whole mission in life. Every time I did push-ups for having the lowest score on a math test. Every cold shower I took for being the last guy to make it to gym. Every time I missed a meal. *Every* time, I consoled myself by thinking about standing up there in front of all the famous old grads of The Arsenal, in front of all the mothers and fathers, in front of the whole student body. Loading the gun. Feeling the rod tamping down the powder. Feeling the familiar heft of the stock against my shoulder. Setting the sight on the red circle of the target.

And pulling the trigger.

Ka-pow!

Kiss my ass, all of you Achievers and Winners and *rigor et disciplina* jerks—kiss my ass all of you. *Because I'm First Shot!*

• • •

I walked out of Crandall House all sweaty and flustered. Part of it was the hundred push-ups Dad had assigned me. But there was something else. I had this weird floaty feeling. It was like everything seemed kind of transparent. Like nothing was real exactly.

This was it. I had lost my chance.

I was a worm forever. A vestige. An appendix. A nothing. The line of Great Crandalls had dwindled and dwindled over the years until all that was left was me. Worm Crandall.

As I was leaving, I noticed this ridiculously babelicious girl walking briskly past me. She wore the school uniform— a khaki skirt, a green shirt, penny loafers. She had to be new because I didn't recognize her. Her hair was up in a ponytail, swishing back and forth on her shoulders. I walked behind her, feeling like I was hypnotized. Swish. Swish. Swish. Suddenly she stopped, like she had changed her mind about where she was going.

I banged into her. I don't know what it was about her, but she was really solid. Like hitting a brick wall. I nearly fell down. As I grabbed at her, trying to keep from falling down, somehow my right hand kind of ended up right on her left boob. Which, I have to tell you, was a pretty nice boob, too.

The girl had very large, very cold green eyes and wore a lot of makeup. At The Arsenal a girl might wear a little eyeliner and maybe even a tiny bit of blush—if they were totally into their looks. But anything beyond that was considered seriously tacky. This girl, though, had her whole face painted up like she was a model about to do a photo shoot.

"You ever try watching where you're going, you pervert?" she said. She had about the drippiest Southern accent I'd ever heard. Then she yanked my hand off her boob. Her fingernails were long and red.

"Sorry," I mumbled. "Really sorry."

We were so close together that I could see every detail of her face. I wondered why she wore so much makeup. Everything about her was perfect—her mouth, her skin, her teeth. I'm not the kind of guy who exaggerates: she just didn't have any flaws. Her breath smelled like mint chewing gum.

"Moron!" she said. Except she pronounced it "*moe*-ron." She pushed past me.

This was supposed to be the day of my big triumph. But it was turning out to be the day of my biggest humiliation.

I wanted to die.

4

But while we're on the subject of dying . . .

On July ninth, a little over two years ago, the police chief from the town of Dartington, Maine, came to our house and knocked on the door. It was raining hard, a frigid rain, unseasonably cold. On a day like that, even police chiefs stayed home.

My dad answered the door. "Um . . ." Chief Dowd said.

"What is it, Emil?"

Chief Dowd had water streaming down his face. It almost looked like he'd been crying. "Mr. Crandall," he said. "There's been an accident."

After that, my life was never the same.

The "accident" turned out to be a murder. My mom's body was found out on the Barrens, half a mile from the road. I was never told any specifics. Dad just told me that she'd been murdered.

"How?" I said. "By who?"

"By *whom*," he said.

"By *whom*, okay, by *whom*?"

But Dad just shook his head. Then he walked away, went into his office, and closed the door. I lay out there on the floor by myself and cried. I had had this huge argument with Mom that afternoon—which was kind of unusual because Mom and I didn't fight that much. It wasn't just the fact that she was dead that made me feel bad. But the thought that the last thing I had done with my mother was to call her a bunch of bad names—it made me feel so ashamed. Lying there crying on the floor, I couldn't remember what the fight had even been about. Just that the last thing I'd yelled before I grabbed my rifle and stomped out of the house to go practice over at the shooting range was: "I wish you were dead!"

I cried and cried. And Dad didn't comfort me at all, he just stayed there, locked in his office.

Weird as it may seem—we never talked about Mom's death again. Not once.

The Dartington Rifles mustered out at 1530 hours.

(The Arsenal was a military academy, like, a hundred and fifty years ago, but pretty soon after the Civil War it was converted into a normal prep school. In keeping with our Grand Traditions, though, we've kept all this dumb military stuff. You don't start something, you "muster out." And time's always expressed like "class starts at oh seven thirty hours"—same as in the army.)

Anyway, I got there at 1537 hours. Everybody was lined up at attention, wearing their practice uniform—blue pants and shirts, blue baseball caps. They were all waiting on me. Which meant I immediately got smacked with fifty push-ups and a big speech from Colonel Taylor about how we were supposed to be role models and all that crap.

What did I care? I was just the stupid alternate.

Once I was done with the push-ups, I joined the line. Colonel Taylor made us stand at attention while he walked up and down in front of us, eyeballing everybody and chewing on his cigar. Then finally he said, "Ladies and gentlemen, I have an announcement to make. This morning at approximately twelve hundred hours, Mr. Willets, your fellow Dartington Rifles member, made the altogether chickenshit decision to take his own life by means of swallowing large quantities of sleeping pills." Colonel Taylor used to be in the army and talked like he'd watched that movie *Patton* way too many times. "Had he used a more manly and effective device such as a firearm, he would doubtless have been successful. Being the pathetic loser that he is, however, Mr. Willets failed. He is still alive."

Which all seemed a little harsh to me—even for Colonel Taylor. But in the back of my mind, I realized that Willets's misfortune might be my good luck.

"Mr. Willets's parents have removed him from the school," Colonel Taylor continued. "Good riddance, I say. As a result, Mr. Crandall is now an official member of the team. Congratulations, Mr. Crandall."

He stepped forward and shook my hand.

I felt something jump in my chest. Willets. Poor old Willets was one of these guys who always seemed stressed to the breaking point. But at that moment I would be lying if I told you I was feeling sorry for him. I just felt glad. Does that make me a bad person? I don't know. But it's how I felt. It meant I still had my dream. I still had a chance to be First Shot.

Colonel Taylor told us to left face. Then he marched us over to the shooting range. As we marched, I noticed a brown ponytail hanging out of one of the baseball caps. Swish. Swish. Swish.

Oh, *no*! I couldn't believe it. It was that new girl, the one who'd called me a moron for feeling up her boob. Since she was the only person on the team I didn't know, it meant she had to be CLEARY, M.—the girl who'd beaten my ass at the qualifying shoot. This was just the worst thing that could possibly happen in the world. At least it seemed that way at that moment.

We reached the range, then Colonel Taylor started us shooting. After that, he went away. It's rumored that Colonel Taylor has a slight drinking problem. Whatever the case, he's not exactly the most hands-on shooting coach.

We just lined up and banged away at the targets for a while. The rifles shot black powder, so there was this giant cloud of smoke around us.

After a while the wind picked up and the smoke cleared. A couple minutes earlier Garrett Rothenberg had been shooting right next to me. Now he was gone.

A pair of large green eyes looked at me. It was her— CLEARY, M. I wondered what the M stood for.

"What are you *doing*?" she said, looking at me like I was a total idiot.

"Huh?" I said. Because I'm a lady-killer, I always know the coolest possible thing to say.

"Your rifle. You don't hold it like *that*."

"What are you talking about?" I was holding the rifle like I always hold a rifle.

"Your rifle. You need to support it, like this." She wrapped the sling around her arm really tightly, then kind of jammed the base of her hand up under the stock.

"I've shot like this for years. It works fine."

"You're Crandall, right?"

"Yeah. So?"

"Look," she drawled, "I saw your qualifying score. I don't care if these other *moe*-rons can't shoot. But I need a little competition here. If you don't at least halfway learn to shoot right, I'll start getting lazy out here."

"Halfway learn to—" I felt my face flush with anger. "I can shoot rings around these guys."

"Yeah, but compared to me?" She shrugged and batted her eyes. "Compared to me, I hate to tell you, but you pretty much suck."

My eyes widened. I was about to say something back to her—something real biting and smart that would hurt her feelings—but I couldn't really think of anything like that. So I just kind of stammered and made stupid noises.

And then Colonel Taylor came out and told us to line up. His eyes looked a little watery and he seemed to be walking very carefully, like he was trying to keep everybody from thinking he was drunk.

We marched back to the quad. I kept watching CLEARY, M.'s ponytail in front of me. Swish. Swish. Swish.

After Colonel Taylor dismissed us, I started to walk back to my room. But then someone called to me. "Hey! Crandall!" I turned. It was CLEARY, M., looking at me. "Meet me here tomorrow morning at six o'clock." Like she was commanding me.

"Me?" I pointed at my chest. "What for?"

"I'm gonna show you some stuff."

"Like what?"

"I told you, somebody needs to show you how to shoot right."

"I shoot fine."

She narrowed her green eyes. "And listen to me. Listen hard. This isn't a hookup. Okay? You're not my type. So don't even get your hopes up."

"What is your type?" I said. Trying to sound cheeky or something, I guess.

She smacked her chewing gum a couple of times, her perfect jaw moving up and down as she looked at me with her cold green eyes. Not exactly like she was disgusted. But like I was barely worthy of notice.

"Not you," she said.

Then she turned around and swished away.

As I turned to go, Garrett Rothenberg looked at me and said, "Misty from Mississippi."

"What?"

He pointed at CLEARY, M. "Annie Oakley. Her name's Misty. Love it, huh? Misty? Sounds like a porn star from the eighties."

I shrugged.

"You watch," Rothenberg said. "By midterms? I'm gonna be wearing that chick like a Hong Kong tattoo."

"You're a douche bag," I said.

He grinned. "Watch me work, baby. Watch me work."

5

I read what they said in the papers after Mom was killed. They made some subtle innuendos about my dad being a suspect. They talked about "a history of marital difficulties between the couple" and "aspects of the crime which pointed to The Arsenal" and some other stuff like that. Nothing real blatant.

But then the whole thing just faded away.

For a long time I thought about Mom every day. Things between me and Dad had always been a little distant. Dad's kind of a by-the-book guy. There's a right way and a wrong way to do everything. Whatever I did, it always seemed like it wasn't good enough. Mom, on the other hand, seemed to always find something about me to encourage, something to praise.

She was an artist. Not professionally. She actually worked part-time in the accounting department for The Arsenal. But she'd studied art in college, and she was always drawing. If I colored outside the lines, she said I showed excellent expression. Whereas Dad would just say, "You colored outside the lines, David. Might want to clean that up a little."

Dad had always ridden me pretty hard once I started going to school at The Arsenal. It was the whole not-showing-favoritism thing. Okay, that's cool. I understand he can't look like he's playing favorites with his kid. But after Mom died, he took it to a whole new level. Every tiny infraction of school rules, every minor failure, every moment of mediocrity, gave him a chance to grind me. More push-ups, more disappointed looks, more grimaces, more cold showers, more missed meals. The push-ups and stuff—hey, who cares? I can deal.

It was the constant feeling of disapproval that started wearing me down. Before Mom died, he'd been tough. But the constant look of disappointment on his face—that was new. So what happened? My grades started dropping. My attitude started getting worse. I just stopped caring.

The only thing I kept being interested in was making First Shot.

And Dad? I just tried to keep my head down and avoid him. After a while I got pretty good at it. I got to where I just sort of stopped taking up space. I was like a ninja—invisible in plain sight.

And so I started to forget about Mom.

Until last week.

• • •

During the school year I always live in one of the dorms. But during the summer I live at home. Last Monday was the second-to-last day of the summer.

I was sitting downstairs playing PlayStation when someone knocked on the door. I paused the game and answered the door. It was Chief Dowd, from Dartington, the town that the school is located near.

"Hi," I said.

"Hello, son," Chief Dowd said. He was a middle-aged guy with a droopy gray mustache that covered up most of his mouth, and eyes that looked kind of sad all the time. "Is your pa in?"

Nobody at The Arsenal would ever refer to their father as "pa." But in Dartington, that was pretty normal. It was a hick town, big-time.

"He's upstairs in his office," I said.

"I'll see myself up," the chief said.

Something about it seemed odd. The chief had been the guy who investigated Mom's murder, so there had been a time when I saw him a lot. But then he just pretty much disappeared. I figured maybe some kid from the school got picked up in town for trying to buy beer or cigarettes or something. I have to admit, I was a little curious. So I snuck up the stairs after the chief and stood near the door of Dad's office.

I couldn't make out much that he said. But I heard the words "new information" several times. That and "consent to search."

Then Dad's voice started getting louder. "No!" he said. "I will *not* consent to that!"

The chief talked some more in his usual soft tone of voice. And my dad's voice kept getting louder.

Finally the door opened. I pretended like I just happened to be walking by.

The chief didn't seem to notice. He just brushed by me and headed down the stairs.

"You do what you have to do!" my father yelled after him. Which was weird, because Dad almost never raises his voice.

That night at dinner I asked Dad why the chief had come to the house.

Dad just shook his head. "He's just trying to throw his weight around," he said. Which didn't seem like a straight answer to me.

But then Dad got up, took his dishes into the kitchen, and dumped all his food in the trash. He'd barely eaten anything.

In the middle of the night I woke up suddenly with my heart beating hard. I couldn't figure out what it was, but for some reason I had this overwhelming feeling that something wasn't right.

I sat up, ears straining, trying to see if I could hear anything.

Then I heard it. *Bump. Bump-ba-bump.*

Someone was in the house!

Could it just be Dad? I looked at my clock. The glowing red numbers told me it was 1:38 A.M. It had to be Dad, right? People didn't break into people's houses at The Arsenal.

"Dad?" I called softly.

No answer. I listened for the noise.

Nothing.

My heart slowed a little. I climbed quietly out of bed, knocked softly on Dad's door. "Dad?" I whispered.

If Dad had gotten up to get a snack or something, he would have turned on some lights.

Bump. Bump-ba-bump.

There it was again. My heart sped up again. It was deep in the house. Maybe down in the basement. Our house—the official headmaster's residence—had been built over a hundred years ago. It was large and drafty. And the basement was extremely creepy.

I pushed Dad's door open. The bed was empty. It hadn't even been slept in, the sheets all crisp and neat.

What in the world was going on? Dad went to bed faithfully every night at ten o'clock, the official lights-out time for the school.

I went back to my room, picked up the camping knife that Dad had given me last Christmas, then crept slowly down the stairs.

Klunk!

I froze halfway down the stairs.

Footsteps were coming up the stairs from the basement. I thought about what I was going to do if it was an intruder.

The door to the basement opened slowly. A dark figure moved out into the room. It took me a minute to see that it was Dad. There was something furtive about the way he moved—like he was trying not to make much noise. I didn't move.

Dad had a shovel in one hand and something else in his other. Something long and thin, wrapped in plastic.

I don't know why I didn't say anything to him. But there was something about his body language that told me he didn't want to be seen or heard or interrupted in whatever he was doing. He opened the front door, then suddenly froze and looked around as though he'd heard something. A ray of light caught his face. He was sweating hard, and his eyes were wide open, nervous-looking. He didn't move for a long, long time.

Then, as though he'd made some kind of decision, he disappeared into the darkness.

As soon as he was gone, I ran up the stairs, pulled on a pair of jeans, went back down, and slipped quietly out the front door of our house.

It was a typical August night. Slightly cool, the air damp. The moon was out, but half concealed behind dark clouds. The imposing black shapes of the various buildings of The Arsenal surrounded me.

In the distance I saw a small figure disappear around the corner of Crandall House, heading in the direction of the athletic fields. I doubted he was going for a late-night jog. Beyond the athletic fields there was nothing. Nothing but the Barrens.

The Barrens. The Arsenal was built on a little spit of land poking out into the Atlantic Ocean, a piece of land so bare and worthless that you couldn't grow anything there, so rocky that no one built houses there. The Arsenal had originally been built by the state of Massachusetts (back when Maine was still part of the Massachusetts colony) to defend against the British. But the land beyond it had been more or less ignored forever. It was desolate and wind-whipped and dangerous. There were a lot of places you could fall or slip, where you'd get trapped, places where the tide came up fast and covered the rocks, beating them with the heavy surf and the fast-moving tide.

It was where they found my mom.

I ran across the quad, past Crandall House, and caught sight of Dad again. Sure enough, he was heading off the track field, out into the Barrens.

I realized too late that I didn't have a flashlight. The footing out in the Barrens was often slippery and unsure. I was going to have to depend on moonlight. But with the sliver of moon appearing and disappearing behind the clouds, it was going to be tricky to keep up with Dad. For a minute I thought about just going back to the house.

Why should I care if Dad wanted to take a walk out here?

Only . . . I knew he wasn't just taking a walk. You didn't bring a shovel on a walk.

After Dad disappeared over a small rocky outcropping, I ran across the track field. The wind was coming in fast off the ocean, and the clouds in the sky looked threatening, like they might bring rain.

Once I got to the edge of the field I slowed down. I could hear the surf now, a dull relentless thudding—and underneath it a harsh grinding noise, like a giant gnashing its teeth, as the waves stirred the big boulders that lay along the surf's edge.

I walked carefully over the rise. It was composed of dark rocks, slippery on their northern sides from the algae that formed where the light didn't hit them. I slipped once, banging my leg against a sharp rock. It hurt like crazy, but I just picked myself up and moved on.

Maybe a hundred yards ahead of me, a tiny light wobbled and wiggled. He must have turned on a flashlight. I couldn't see Dad at all now, not in the tangle of dark rocks. But I could follow the light.

I tried to keep up, but since I didn't have a flashlight and Dad did, he was able to move quicker than I could.

Eventually, I lost track of the light. Now I was alone. I kept moving forward through the rocks. For a couple of minutes the moon came out and I could see fine. But then a big long wall of blackness loomed up out of the dark and covered the moon completely. It was a storm cloud for sure.

The sound of the surf grew louder, the gnashing of the rocks more terrifying. I was climbing now, climbing into a rock-filled darkness. Every kid I knew had come out here and played occasionally. I'd spent a lot of time goofing around in the Barrens myself, back when I was still in elementary school. But that had been during the day.

And even then I don't think I'd ever gone quite this far.

Now I could see almost nothing. I was reduced to feeling my way along. I felt a humming of fear in my blood and I kept thinking, *Go back! Go back!* But something drew me along and I couldn't stop.

The rain hit me a couple of minutes later, the wind whipping at my clothes. I moved forward inch by painful inch, hearing the surf to my left, but not knowing quite how close to the water I was. Suddenly there was a flash of lightning. In the brief flash of light, my heart almost stopped. I was clinging to the side of a cliff! I was on a ledge not more than a foot or two across. To my right was solid rock. To my left, nothing but air.

I was at least a hundred feet above the water, just inches from the edge. Below me the sea boiled, white foam and giant crooked black rocks. If I fell, I'd probably be smashed to pieces. And even if I somehow miraculously survived, the ocean would bash me against the rocks and drown me. And even if I managed to swim out, I knew that the rushing water would carry me past the tip of the point, out into the eight-foot waves, and into the deep ocean. The water in Maine, even in August, is in the fifties. It would be a contest between hypothermia and drowning.

A fall from there was a death sentence. It was that simple.

Would I have gone over the edge if that lightning bolt hadn't flashed when it did? I don't think so. But I might have.

Another flash of lightning. The massive white waves seemed to be reaching up toward me.

This is crazy! I thought. *Just turn around and go back.*

Did I mention that I don't like heights?

Okay, well, I don't. Heights scare the crap out of me. When I was a kid, I could barely even climb a tree. Now, here I was a hundred feet up on the edge of a slippery rock cliff, with wind snatching at me.

Problem was, it was so dark now that going back wasn't much of an option either. Besides, going back would be just as scary as going forward. For a minute I was paralyzed. Couldn't even move. But I realized I had to do *something*. Otherwise I'd freeze and fall in anyway.

So I got down on my hands and knees, put my hands on the edge of the slippery rock, and began crawling, literally inching my way along the cliff edge. I don't know how long I crawled, or how far. But it seemed like forever. It was the most frightening thing I had ever done in my life. And yet there was something strangely exciting about it, too.

It seemed so much more intense and serious out here. I couldn't think about any of the dopey junk that seemed so important back at The Arsenal. My moderately crappy GPA, my moderately okay test scores, my moderately bad class rank. Not even my shooting. All I could think about was moving forward. And not falling off the cliff.

The cold rain stung my skin, hammered my clothes, poured into my eyes. The wind pushed and pulled at me. I was like a slug, inching forward with nothing to guide me but feel. I kept my left hand right at the cliff edge, the tips of my fingers clutching at the rock. As long as I knew where the edge was, I couldn't go over it. Right?

After a while the ledge began to widen. And then the cliff face to my left disappeared, and I found myself on a wide, flat piece of rock. *I'd made it!*

And then, suddenly, another flash of lightning.

In front of me was giant pile of rock. But this was not a natural formation. It was man-made—a low, ruined tower. Years ago some of the local inhabitants used to come out on moonless nights and hoist lanterns to the top of the tower. They would then pull them slowly up and down to simulate lanterns hanging from the yardarms of ships. The idea was to lure hapless freighters against the rocks, where they would be destroyed. The locals would then plunder the boats, stealing anything of value. These plunderers were called "jackstaffs" after the pole on which flags were raised on old sailing ships.

There were still several families in the town of Dartington whose last name was Jackstaff. They all traced their lineage back to the jackstaffs who'd lured ships onto the rocks. They were basically a bunch of mean hicks who spent a lot of time in jail and worked as little as they could. Although I should say in fairness that when I was a kid, my best friend, Leo, was a Jackstaff. But he was like the exception that proves the rule.

Anyway, they called this ruin Jackstaff Tower. I'd never seen it except from the water. Everybody had always said there was only one way to get there without getting killed. And that only the Jackstaffs knew the way.

Apparently somewhere along the way my dad had learned the route. And I guess I'd blundered into it.

Another flash of lightning lit up the tower. Silhouetted against it was the figure of a man. It was Dad. To the left of the tower was a small depression that was filled with sand. My dad was digging furiously.

He wasn't more than twenty feet from me. I slid backward a little so that if he happened to turn around when a flash of lightning went off, he wouldn't see me.

Every minute or two, there would be a flash of light, and Dad would appear again, digging like somebody had put a gun to his head, the water streaming down his face, his dark hair matted against his skull.

And then there was a lull, the rain slackening, the lightning tailing off. I lay in the cold puddle in the total darkness, waiting to see what happened next. It continued to rain—not hard, but steady. I began to shiver.

Finally there was another flash. Dad was lowering something into the hole.

Darkness.

I tried to listen for the sound of his shovel. But with the wind and the surf and the rain, it was impossible to make it out.

Lightning flashed again—this time distantly. Jackstaff Tower hung in the air above me, a black shape against the eerily lit clouds.

Where Dad had been digging was only a sodden pile of sand.

And Dad himself?

He was gone.

6

So that was a week ago.

At 5:50 the alarm went off.

I lay there looking at the clock thinking: *Why did I agree to meet her at this ridiculous hour?* And then I remembered that I hadn't really agreed to anything.

Misty Cleary had just commanded me to show up. Who did she think she was, telling me what to do?

What was I—some kind of lapdog? Just because she was ridiculously beautiful and could shoot the eyes off a fly at fifty paces, she thought I'd come running whenever she called? Don't think so, baby. *I'll show her who's boss!* I rolled back over in the bed and covered my head with my blanket.

Ten minutes later I was waiting by the athletic field, looking at my watch. Another ten minutes went by. Fifteen. Twenty.

Just as I was about to leave, a tall figure in a skirt appeared from Prendergast House, walking briskly toward me. Her ponytail swished from side to side.

"You're late," I said.

"Had to take a shower," she said. Her hair was still wet, and she smelled of soap. Her face was perfectly made up. She took her rifle out of its case. "So they call you Worm, huh?"

"You can call me Mr. Crandall," I said.

She laughed, then held up her rifle. "First thing, we're gonna have to modify the rifles. These things aren't pillar bedded, so when they heat up, they'll stop grouping decently. But that's for later. Second thing, we need to start shooting at a hundred meters. Right now we're doing this fifty-yard stuff. Which is a joke. Fifty yards is for babies."

"No problem," I said.

"But the main thing, you're gonna have to totally relearn your shooting technique."

"Why?"

"I watched you yesterday."

"You did?" I felt this little burst of excitement knowing that she'd actually been paying attention to me in some way or other.

She grimaced, looking disgusted. "Oh, *please*," she said, "don't get all queer on me. I wasn't checking out your abs."

"Whatever," I said.

"Yeah, whatever *whatever*. Point is, I was trying to figure out what kind of technique you shoot." She frowned, narrowed her eyes slightly, looked at me like I was a math problem she was trying to solve. "You don't have any technique at all, do you?"

"What do you mean?"

"I mean . . . you just point at the target and shoot."

I stared at her blankly and sighed really loudly. "What else *would* you do?"

She shook her head. "This is gonna be worse than I thought," she said.

"What?"

"Look," she said. "I'm gonna be shooting in the national black-powder shooting finals in Kentucky in the spring. Your job is gonna be to keep me on my toes." She glared at me. "Now listen up, Worm! If you don't do exactly what I tell you to do, you'll never be good enough to push me. And if you don't push me, I'm gonna lose, come next March. And, honey, that ain't an option."

"Ain't?" I smirked. Nobody said *ain't* at The Arsenal, not even as a joke.

She took out her rifle. It was some kind of strange, funky-looking thing that barely resembled the old-fashioned rifles we used. It still had a ramrod and a percussion cap. But everything else about it looked hypermodern.

"Load your rifle," she said.

"My gun's already loaded."

"A *gun*," she said, making a face like I'd just farted really loudly, "is a shotgun. This is a rifle. If you refer to it again as a 'gun,' I'm going to vomit on you."

I just stood there.

"What are you waiting for," she said, pointing at the target. "Shoot!"

I lifted the rifle to my shoulder, waited until the target appeared in the sight at the end of the rifle, and squeezed the trigger. The was a satisfying *shhhhhh-crack* and a hard impact on my shoulder. I waited until the smoke cleared. In front of me there was a perfect hole, dead center of the target.

I smiled broadly.

She shook her head sadly. "Man, oh, man," she said. "I really got my work cut out for me."

"What! It's a perfect bull's-eye!"

"That's not the point," she said. "You did it wrong. Based on how you shoot? You're maxed out. I bet you haven't gotten any better in the last two years, have you?"

I cleared my throat. She was right. But so what?

"The way you shoot, there's no way for you to get any better. It's impossible. You have to start from scratch. Totally."

"That's dumb!"

"What if I told you I could get you a perfect ten out of ten at fifty yards?" she said. "I mean, not just sometimes. I mean, every single time."

"That's ridiculous," I said. "Nobody's ever shot like that in the history of The Arsenal. Well . . . except for Elliot Crandall the Third back in 1861."

"Watch," she said.

She lifted her rifle, fired. The target twitched slightly. But there was no new hole.

"You missed," I said.

She shook her head. "Go look."

I shrugged, walked all the way out to the target, checked. There was the slight tear at one edge of the circular hole in the paper target. She'd shot smack through the center of my circle.

I walked back. "Okay," I said.

For the next eight minutes, she loaded and fired. The target continued to twitch each time she fired. But the hole never got bigger. I couldn't believe it. Each time she was shooting straight through the hole I'd made. It wasn't just that she was shooting better than me. She was shooting better than I even imagined it was *possible* to shoot.

After she'd fired ten times she set her rifle down, crossed her arms, and looked at me, smacking away on her gum. Her cold green eyes bored straight into me. My cheeks flushed. I felt like the world's biggest loser. I could never beat her. Never. The only way I'd ever make First Shot was to shoot her in the head.

"Okay," I said sullenly. "I'm listening."

7

Man, was I in a bad mood for the rest of the day! Misty spent about an hour picking apart my shooting technique. *Move your hand here, put your eye there, do this, do that.* By the end I was shooting worse than I'd shot when I was in seventh grade. And her attitude? Totally irritating, totally condescending. By the end I'd forgotten she was the best-looking girl I'd ever met. I just hated her. Pure and simple.

In pre-calc, I flunked the pop quiz, even though I was sure I knew how to do everything. In AP history, I sat there blatantly reading a book, not even hiding it, until Mr. Greener made me do push-ups. Then in English, the only class I really liked, I picked a fight with Mr. Entwhistle about *Hamlet*. I said Hamlet was a "wimpy dumb-ass sissy who was too much of a wuss to do what it takes."

Bam. More push-ups.

Mr. Entwhistle dismissed the class as I was finishing my push-ups. When I was done, I just lay there in the empty room feeling the gritty floor on my cheek.

"Come to my office, would you, Mr. Crandall," Mr. Entwhistle said. He stood up, grabbed his cane, and started walking.

I followed him back to his office, which was on the bottom floor of the building. Mr. Entwhistle had something wrong with his leg, so he walked with a cane, just leaning on it like crazy, and it took forever to get there. But finally we reached the ground floor and he opened the door with an ancient key, and let me into the office. It was like Dad's office—paneled in mahogany and furnished with old wooden furniture—only a lot smaller. It smelled like pipe smoke.

I sat down in the old leather chair, fiddled with a crack in the red leather seat cushion while Mr. Entwhistle leaned his gnarled old cane against the desk, then filled his pipe with tobacco. He was an old guy, probably like sixty, who wore a white beard stained yellow from the pipe smoke. But somehow he didn't seem like an old guy. He had very piercing blue eyes, and was probably the best teacher I'd ever had.

"Isn't it illegal to smoke inside the building or something?" I said.

Mr. Entwhistle just looked at me with his blue eyes and sucked on his pipe. "You're not wrong," he said finally. "About Hamlet, I mean."

I kept fiddling with the crack in the leather, sticking my finger in it, feeling the soft stuffing inside the cushion.

"Lost your convictions?" he said. "You seemed quite sure of yourself ten minutes ago."

I shrugged. "I don't really give a shit about Hamlet," I said. I guess I was just trying to get him pissed off, pick a fight like I did in class. But it didn't work. Most teachers if you cussed around them, they'd get all hot and bothered and you'd lose hot showers for a while. But Mr. Entwhistle, now that he wasn't in class, he didn't seem to even notice.

"Hamlet's father was murdered by his uncle," Mr. Entwhistle said. "It's easy to say, 'Hey, pal, you need to go out there, kick ass, take names.' Hm? But in real life, it's not that easy. Is it? Real life's a lot more complicated."

I kept sticking my finger in the crack, going deeper and deeper. The stuffing had a soft, almost slick feeling.

"You ever talk about your mother's murder with anybody?" he said. "A friend? A shrink? Your father? Anybody?"

I shrugged. Dad had sent me to this counselor for a while. But the guy was a big phony who smiled all the time and tried to joke around with you and be cool. He'd rap knuckles with you and tell you about all these supposedly cool bands he was listening to. It was all like chapter one of the shrink manual: *How to Break the Ice with a Teenager.* Honestly, the guy gave me the creeps. After a while I stopped going.

"I take that to mean no," Mr. Entwhistle said.

I said nothing.

"Look, I'm sure you heard the rumors."

"What rumors?"

He cocked his head, looked at me curiously. "That it was your father who killed her."

I'd heard whispers, sure. And, like I say, the papers had implied it. "Yeah."

Mr. Entwhistle sucked on his pipe a little. It made a tiny whistling noise. "He didn't do it, you know."

Again I didn't say anything.

"You're getting to be a big boy," Mr. Entwhistle said. "I think it's only right, only fair for you to hear another perspective about your mother. I've known you since you were born. I know you and your mother had a special attachment. And I'm sure that now that she's gone you've probably romanticized her a bit."

"I can't help it if my dad's a jerk," I said.

"I'm not talking about your father. I'm talking about Katharine."

That was my mom's name. Katharine Boyce Crandall.

"I've been here almost forty years now," Mr. Entwhistle said. "I knew your mother from the time she was born, too. As you know, her father was the headmaster here before your dad." He smiled for a moment, like he was thinking back. "She was always a beautiful child. She sparkled. She was full of life. And she attracted men from the time she was . . . well, from probably way too early in her life."

There's stuff you really don't want to hear about your mother. I mean, I knew she was beautiful. But . . . it's not something you exactly want to dwell on, you know what I mean?

Mr. Entwhistle continued. "I'm going to tell you a story.

It's something that only a few people know. And I happen to be one of them." He diddled with his pipe, tapping it on the desk, adjusting it somehow, then started smoking it again. "Your grandfather, Grantland Boyce, was headmaster of The Arsenal from 1964 until 1991. He was a brilliant guy. Funny. Warm. He probably could have been a great scholar, taught at Harvard, all that stuff. But for whatever reason, he ended up here. But he wasn't just a garden-variety head-master, doing his little thing at the school. He wrote books about education and how to motivate young people. He was on TV. He lectured across the country. He was a natural performer, a truly great speaker."

Mr. Entwhistle's voice trailed off. I couldn't figure out what in the world he was talking about.

"So what I'm getting at is that your mother grew up here around this man who was revered—almost worshipped. In many ways, The Arsenal was almost an extension of Grant-land Boyce. It's not as bad with your father. He doesn't have the same presence here that Grantland did. But you can understand how your mother must have felt. When your dad's headmaster—well, it's a little suffocating, isn't it?"

"A *little*?" I said. *Suffocating* was not the right word. It totally, totally sucked.

Mr. Entwhistle smiled. "Your mother, I mean, she just *burned* to get out of here. She went off to college at the Rhode Island School of Design—which is one of the best art schools in the country. I remember seeing her come back from college at Christmas that first year. She had gone away as this little girl. And she came back . . ." He cleared his throat. "Let's just say she blossomed. All the male teachers, they could barely keep their eyes inside their heads. Your father was twenty-two that year. He'd just graduated from Yale and he had come back here, I suppose, to kill a couple of years before he went off and fulfilled his destiny. But, boy, let me tell you, he noticed your mother. And she noticed him. Two years later your mom dropped out of college and married your father.

"They were the golden couple here. Good-looking, smart, talented. By then your father had been named dean. Twenty-four years old! It was unprecedented. But as you know, he's a very industrious fellow. And frankly, private school faculties are not exactly dripping with practical, industrious people. Grantland took your father under his wing and quickly your father became his right-hand man. This would have been around 1990, I guess."

I yawned. If Mr. Entwhistle was trying to bore the snot out of me, he was doing a pretty good job. I *so* did not care about the history of The Arsenal.

"But at that point your father made it quite clear he was only going to stay on for another year, and after that he was going to leave The Arsenal and go to graduate school. Then, suddenly, at Christmas in 1990, it was revealed that the school was having severe financial problems. Your father let it be known that he was going to stick around for an extra year to help out. But then he was absolutely, totally, completely going to leave The Arsenal.

"Meanwhile, your father and mother were having a few problems. One time this folksinger came to Dartington to play at the pub down there. Your mother went to see him. Next thing you know, she was gone. Went back to New York City with the folksinger." Mr. Entwhistle stroked his beard. "I'm not trying to shock you, or make you think the worse of your mother. But, as you'll see, I'm going somewhere with this."

"Mm-hm," I said, poking around in the seat cushion some more. I knew Mom and Dad had gone through a couple of rough patches. But it was something I'd tried not to think about.

"Your mom came back, of course. The fact is, she really loved your father. But she made it clear that she was not going to stay here much longer, that Katharine Crandall was made for bigger things than The Arsenal. She was painting furiously. There was some talk about an exhibition in New York—though that never quite jelled. She wore a ring in her nose, and her skirts were a lot shorter than those that were allowed by the dress code.

"Then one day Grantland Boyce resigned. Bam. Just like that. And just as quickly, the board of directors convened. When they walked out of the room five hours later, your father was the headmaster of The Arsenal. After that there was no more talk of graduate school. And your mother, she was pregnant. With you. That was the end of her art career. I don't think she made a serious attempt to paint a picture after you were born."

"That's not true!" I said. "She painted all the time."

"Sure. Finger painting, sketching, piddling around. But nothing finished, nothing serious, nothing that would get her an exhibition in New York. Oh, she *talked* about it. There was always a plan, always a serious thing she was working on, always talk about how many job offers your dad had to take over a school in Manhattan or Boston, always complaints about how boring and parochial it was here. She wanted to get out of town *so* bad! But it was just talk. She never did anything."

I sighed loudly.

"Grantland Boyce stole the endowment."

"Huh?" I said. I didn't get what he was talking about.

"Your grandfather stole 24.6 million dollars from the endowment of The Arsenal. Over the course of several years. By the time it was discovered, the school was almost broke. If it hadn't been for the financial problems, your father would have left. But Grantland Boyce had finally used it all up. He couldn't hide it any longer. The school was about to die.

"Your father saved this school. He had been accepted to graduate school. He was ready to hit the road, head off toward his glorious destiny. And the directors came to him when they finally discovered the situation the school was in.

They begged your father to stay. *Begged* him. And finally he agreed."

I had never heard any of this. All I knew was that my grandfather—Mom's father—had died soon after he stopped being headmaster of the school. I don't know if I'd ever specifically been told that he killed himself. But it was always my impression that he did.

"What did he do with all that money?" I said.

Mr. Entwhistle shrugged. "Nobody knows. They never found it."

"Huh," I said. It made me feel dirty somehow. I'd always heard what a great guy Mom's dad was. Now, suddenly, Mr. Entwhistle was putting everything I'd ever been told about him in doubt.

"The rap around here—the story everybody tells—is that your father stuck around here in this backward part of Maine when he could have gone elsewhere, that he dragged your mom down, kept her from pursuing her dreams. The reason that's the rap around here is because your mother told it to everybody. Incessantly. I mean, she was subtle about it, but that was her story. You want to know the truth, though? The reason—the actual, final reason that your father stayed?—it was because your mom convinced him to stay. She knew that if he saved the school, then the directors could avoid publicly acknowledging the fraud and avoid criminal prosecution of *her* father.

"And so that's what he did. It took your father almost a

decade before The Arsenal was truly out of the weeds. And, my God, did he work his ass off."

I started to giggle, but Mr. Entwhistle narrowed his blue eyes at me and the giggle sort of died on my lips.

"Your father raised money, he pinched pennies, he worked out strategies for deferring expenses . . . and eventually he turned this place around. But, oh boy, everybody resents him. There's a long memory in a place like this. Cheapskate. Salary-cutter. Micromanager. Inflexible. No fun. Sound like your dad?"

I gave him a sour smile.

"But see, David, I'm one of the few people who knows the whole story. It was your mom who kept *him* from pursuing *his* dreams. Not the other way around. Before he became responsible for this entire school, he was a much more easygoing, likable guy. Truth is, your mom couldn't stick with anything for five minutes. The thing that made her fun to be around, that made men love her, that made kids think she was cool—that probably made her seem like a much more appealing parent than your father—is the same thing that made her stay here. She lived for the moment. She couldn't stick with a plan to save her soul. She just didn't have what it took to leave."

"So," I said. "What were these big dreams my dad supposedly had?"

"He was going to be a writer."

"A *writer?*" I made a farting noise with my lips. What a joke. I'd never seen Dad write anything longer than a ten-dollar check.

"I taught your father," Mr. Entwhistle said. "He was probably the most talented writer I've had." He paused. "Well . . . other than you."

I frowned. *"Me?"*

"You think I don't see you back there scribbling in those notebooks?"

I flushed. I didn't think anybody knew about my notebooks. I mean . . . people saw me writing. But I always told them I was taking notes in class.

"You dropped one of your notebooks in class once," he said. "I couldn't help myself. I read it. In many ways it reminded me of your father. The same gift for narrative. The same eye for detail. The same ability to see through people."

I felt a rush of anger. I'd never let *anyone* see my notebooks. "That's my personal stuff!" I said.

"I know." Mr. Entwhistle's blue eyes seemed very hard suddenly. "But I read it anyway."

"God!"

"The one about the kid at this private school who wins First Shot and then misses and shoots his father? I thought that one was kind of melodramatic and immature. But the one about the man who kills his wife and buries her under a terrazzo floor?—I thought that was really nice. Really creepy and interesting. What I especially thought was interesting was the way the man's son knows his father did it, but he doesn't do anything about it. It had a . . ." He smiled thinly. "It had a Shakespearean ring to it."

"It's just a freakin' story."

"A story about a wimpy dumb-ass sissy who won't fight for what's right? Who won't do what it takes?"

"Blow me!"

"If you think you can shock me with your potty mouth," Mr. Entwhistle said, "I hate to disappoint you, but I've heard lots worse."

I don't know why, but all of a sudden, I just felt this big explosion of emotion. I felt like I was just gonna blow up and it would be like PPPPPKKKKKKOOOWWWW!!!!!, and The Arsenal would just vaporize and all the lies and bullshit and pain would just blow away into the ocean.

For a second I thought I might start blubbering like a baby. But I didn't. I just sat there staring up in the air, with my eyes feeling all hot.

"Your dad didn't kill your mom," Mr. Entwhistle said for the second time.

"Then who did?"

Mr. Entwhistle shrugged. "We'll probably never know." He set down his pipe, took hold of his cane, and fidgeted with it. Then he sighed loudly. "Look, let me just say it plain. Your mom messed around with a few guys. Some of them were bad guys." He shrugged. "I didn't want to say that to you. But it's a fact."

I wanted to say, *Then why did my dad just sneak off in the middle of the night and bury something in the sand next to Jackstaff Tower? Something that looked a hell of a lot like a rifle?*

But instead I just got up and walked out. And slammed the door really, really hard.

8

So. The notebooks.

I guess I better tell you about the notebooks.

About the time that Mom left Dad for the third time, I started writing these little stories in a notebook. I always knew Mom and Dad had problems. And I guess—even though it pissed me off that Mom left *me* as well as Dad when she'd skip town with some douche-bag guy—I always felt sorry for her, too. She'd come back looking so sad. And then she and Dad would make up and be all gross and kissy-kissy and lovey-dovey.

But it hurt. You know? Having your mom choose some tattooed jerk on a motorcycle over you?—even if she only stayed gone for, like, a week. It just sucked.

And so, when I was in eighth grade and she went off with some guy who'd spent the summer painting buildings around The Arsenal, I picked up this notebook, and this frenzy of creativity just sort of fell on me. I started drawing pictures and writing notes and all of a sudden this story started to appear. It was kind of like one of those Japanese manga books or a graphic novel or something. Not quite a cartoon, but not quite *not*, either.

And the story was about this kid whose mom runs away with some loser on a motorcycle. It had all this wild stuff in it. Ghosts and crazy bikers with machine guns and space aliens . . . It was kind of dumb. But it was fun.

And then Mom came back and that was it for the notebook. Then another time Mom and Dad had this big fight and I started writing. And after that I just always had a notebook. I stopped drawing pictures after a while, just started making up little stories. And the more I hated school, and the more I felt trapped in this musty old place, and the worse my grades got—the more I wrote in my notebook.

After Mom died? Forget about it. For like six months I did nothing but shoot and scribble in my notebook.

After Mr. Entwhistle's class, I went back to my dorm room and lay down on the bed and got out the notebook that he'd been talking about. Then I read over the story about the kid whose dad had wasted his mom.

And it was all right there.

Just like Hamlet, dude. You suspect something—in fact, in your heart you *know* something. But you do squat about it.

I was lying on my bunk when Garrett Rothenberg came in. Roommates are assigned by lottery, so I had no choice in the matter. I couldn't stand the guy. But I was stuck with him.

I quickly swept the notebook off my bed, tossed it on my desk like it was just some boring homework or something.

"Hamlet's a wuss?" he said. "Nice. You know that's what I kept thinking the whole time I read that stupid play? This guy's a wuss. But I'd never say it. Props, bro."

I didn't say anything.

"You know what would have been good?" he said. "If somebody just came out and like stabbed his ass. Right there in the first act, huh? Would have saved me a lot of reading."

I just lay there looking at the bottom of his bunk.

Garrett opened the mini-fridge, rummaged around. "Where's my Red Bull? Did Musgrave steal it again? That ass-muncher. Oh, here it is." He took out a can, popped the top, and started slurping loudly. "Hey, heard you were out shooting with that new chick, Miiiindy from Mississiipppp-piiiiiii." He did a bad Southern accent, dragging out all the syllables.

"It's Misty."

"Misty, Mindy, whatever. I'm gonna be all over her. You watch."

I stood up, grabbed my bicycle, and carried it out the door and into the hallway.

"What's up with *you*, Hamlet?" he said to my back. He laughed his loud obnoxious laugh. *Huh-huh-huh-huh.* "Hamlet! I love it. See you, Hamlet!"

9

I rode out the front gate of The Arsenal, under the old arch with *Rigor et Disciplina* chiseled into the stone, and down the road to the town of Dartington.

It was about five miles—not a bad ride. There's not much to see. A couple of tourist cabins, and then some mobile homes on the right where the Jackstaff clan lives. Back when I was in elementary school I used to be pretty tight with this kid Leo Jackstaff. But then in seventh grade I transferred from public school to The Arsenal, and I didn't see him much after that. But whenever I drove by, I looked to see if he was there. These days he drove this old beat-up Mustang and had a couple tattoos. I heard he dropped out of school after ninth grade.

His old blue Mustang was parked outside the ratty old mobile home where he and his mother lived. But I didn't see him anywhere in the yard.

When I got to the village, I rode up to the city hall, chained my bike to a street sign, and then walked up to the police department office, which was around the back side of the city hall complex.

A cow bell clanked when I walked in.

"May I help you?" the lady behind the counter said.

"I'd like to see Chief Dowd."

She frowned for a moment. "Your name is . . ."

"David. David Crandall."

Her eyes widened suddenly. "Oh, my," she said. "Just a moment."

After a minute the chief came out, looking at me with his sad eyes, his droopy mustache hiding whatever expression was on his lips. "Well, hello, son," he said. "What can I do for you?"

"I want to know what happened," I said. "I want to know everything."

He stroked his mustache. "Come on back," he said finally.

I followed him back to his office, a plain square box of a room with white-painted walls and a bulletin board with wanted posters thumbtacked to it. We sat down in his office and he said, "Does your father know you're here?"

I shook my head.

He looked thoughtful. "This is an in-progress police investigation," he said. "Normally we don't just hand out information willy-nilly."

"You've had two years," I said. "My mom was murdered and in two years nobody's told me squat." Suddenly I felt mad. "That's not right!"

"I'm sure your father was just trying to protect you," he said.

"From what? Somebody shot my mom. What could make it worse?"

Chief Dowd chewed thoughtfully on the ragged fringe of his mustache. "Okay," he said. "What do you want to know?"

"I just said. Everything."

Chief Dowd rested his head on his hands, kept chewing on his mustache. "I don't know, son," he said finally.

"You suspect my dad, don't you?" I said.

He cleared his throat but didn't say anything.

"Where was she found?" I said.

"The Barrens."

"Yeah, but *where* in the Barrens?"

"About a hundred feet in, just off the athletic field."

"Who found her?"

"Some kids."

"What kids?"

"Look—"

"What kids?" I repeated.

"A couple of the Jackstaff boys. Leo and his older brother, Nolan."

"What were they doing there?"

"You know how they are. Hard to get a straight story out of a Jackstaff. They said they were just out messing around. And I saw no reason to disbelieve them."

"Where was she shot?"

"In the chest. The bullet passed right through her heart."

"What kind of bullet?"

"What do you mean, what kind of bullet?"

"Thirty-eight, nine millimeter, thirty caliber? Handgun, rifle, shotgun, what?"

"Large bore. *Very* large."

Large bore. It took a minute to absorb that. Normal modern guns shoot fairly small bullets. The only thing that you would describe as "very large bore" would be . . .

"You're saying she was shot with a black-powder rifle," I said, eyes widening.

He nodded.

"Which means it almost had to be somebody on campus." Everybody on campus had a black-powder rifle—part of the Grand Traditions that went along with gunnery class and First Shot and all that.

"The state of Maine has a black-powder hunting season," the chief said. "There are other people around here who might shoot a big-bore black-powder rifle. But, yeah, the logical conclusion is that it was somebody on campus. It was kind of an investigator's nightmare. Every single kid at The Arsenal owns a black-powder firearm. That's part of the *traditions of the school*." He wiggled his fingers in the air sarcastically. "As you may recall, we interviewed every single kid at The Arsenal, along with every single member of the staff and faculty. We got nowhere."

"Maybe that's because—"

"The Arsenal is its own little world. All of you people out there think you're better than us little peons down here in Dartington. Oh, everybody's polite. But prying useful information out of you people was nearly impossible. I felt like I was stumbling around blind. If we'd had something to go on, maybe . . . But we had nothing."

"Can't you do ballistic tests on all the rifles at the school? On *CSI* they shoot them into this gelatin stuff and then use this microscope-type thing to—"

"Every single kid on the campus has a rifle. That's seven hundred tests. You have any idea how much that would cost?" Chief Dowd laughed, but his mouth didn't seem to be smiling under his mustache. "Still, I tried. I asked the DA for permission to perform a ballistic test on every single rifle. But The Arsenal has a lot of politically connected friends. The district attorney told me I couldn't do it, that I had to have a suspect first."

"And *did* you have a suspect?"

Chief Dowd chewed his mustache some more. "Not really," he said finally.

I could feel my heart beating fast. "Not even my dad?"

More mustache chewing. "Look—" he said finally.

"I've watched *CSI*," I said. "Come on. The husband's always a suspect, right?"

Chief Dowd spread his hands but didn't answer me.

"After two years, you suddenly show up at our house asking to search the property," I said. "You must have found out *something*."

"A confidential informant provided us with credible information leading us to believe that evidence pertaining to the investigation might be obtainable in the headmaster's residence." The way he said it, it sounded like something he'd memorized, some kind of standard speech that he gave a lot.

"Credible information," I said. "But not so credible that you could get a search warrant, huh?"

"Like I say, The Arsenal has a lot of political influence around here."

We sat there looking at each other for a while.

"Are you aware of anything in your home," he said, "anything that might pertain to this investigation?"

I sat there for a minute, my mind going back to that crazy evening a week earlier, when I'd spent the night in the Barrens. Finally I shook my head.

"You're sure?"

I nodded.

He looked at me for a while. "See, son, there's something in your face that tells me different."

I couldn't meet his eyes. I kept going over and over and over the same ground. Could my dad have done it? Really? I mean, he was a pain in the neck, yeah. But . . . a murderer? I just couldn't wrap my mind around it.

"Look," I said finally, "what if I could help you?"

"What's that mean?"

"The Arsenal's a weird place. You just said so yourself. Some guy comes in from off campus, starts asking all kinds of questions? Hey, you might not even know the right questions to ask."

"Are you saying you know the right questions?"

I shrugged. "I miss my mom," I said finally. "I know I'll never get her back. But if I could just—" Suddenly I felt like crying again, just like I did in Mr. Entwhistle's office. But again, I fought it off. "I want to know what happened."

"Even if the answer leads you someplace really . . . hurtful?"

"I want to know what happened," I said again.

He shook his head. "I don't like this. I don't like this at all. You're a minor."

"I can help you!" I said.

Finally he shook his head. "If you have something to tell me, just tell me."

"I'm going to find out," I said. "If you want to help me, fine. If not? I'll do it myself."

He shook his head. "This is not a kid's game."

"A kid's game! I don't have a mother anymore. You think I don't know this isn't a game!"

"Look, I'm sorry," he said. "I didn't mean it that way. I'm just saying that this is a job for professionals."

"Because you've done such a fabulous job of it so far?"

"You got a smart little mouth, don't you?" the chief said.

"What do you need to find out?" I said. "Just tell me what you need to find out. And I'll do what I can."

"I need to know if something has been removed from your home recently."

"I can't tell you that."

"Can't? Or won't?"

"I don't *know*!"

He sighed. "Hold on." He went out of the room and came back about five minutes later with a cardboard box that had CRANDALL written on the side with a blue marker. He set the box on the desk, rummaged through it, pulled out a manila folder, and set it on the desk. I could see that there were a bunch of photographs inside. But he angled it away from me so that I couldn't see what they were pictures of, then started leafing through the photos. Finally he came out with one, set it on the desk in front of me.

"You know what that is?" he said.

I looked at the photograph. It appeared to be a close-up—a piece of blue-and-white fabric. I had a sudden flash. It was a dress Mom had worn a lot.

"That was Mom's dress," I said.

"Not the dress," he said. "This." He pointed at the lower right-hand corner of the photograph.

It was a key. A little steel key, covered with a thin coating of brown rust. It wasn't a normal key, though. It was the old-fashioned kind like you see in old movies, with a round shaft and a flag-shaped thingy at the end. Kind of like the one Mr. Entwhistle used to open his office door. Only smaller and much more complex-looking.

"I don't know," I said. "It looks like some kind of old-fashioned key."

"That doesn't mean anything to you?"

I looked at the picture more closely. The key was lying on a strange, multicolored piece of glass.

"Hold on," I said. "I need to see that." I grabbed the file folder from the chief, pulled it over to me.

"Hey!" he said. "You don't want to see—"

But by then I'd opened it up. And there on the top was a picture of my mom. You could still see it was her—the long brown hair splayed out on the rock, the slim body, the high cheekbones, the blue eyes. She was staring straight up in the air, and there was a red stain in the center of her blue-and-white dress. But there was something strange about her. Not just the fact that her skin was pale and her lips blue. She looked like a wax figure that had started melting.

"Aw, jeez," the chief said. "You didn't need to see that."

I stared at the picture for a while. "Why's she look like that?" I said. "Like she's melting?"

"It was one of those freak things. Right after she was killed, there was a freezing rain. She was completely encrusted in ice."

As soon as he said it, I saw it perfectly. The ice was pretty thick. At least a quarter inch. Lying next to her body was the key that the chief had wanted me to look at. And under the key was what I had taken to be a colored rectangle of glass. Only I realized then that it wasn't glass. It was a painting—a painting covered with ice. There was a vaguely human figure under the ice. But you couldn't make out any detail.

"What happened to the painting?" I said.

"That's not what I'm interested in," the chief said. "Tell me about the key."

"I don't know anything about that," I said. "I just want to see the painting."

He scratched his mustache. "Okay. But I don't think it'll do you much good."

He went out of the room again, came back with another cardboard box. This one was full of paper bags. He opened one, pulled out the key from the photograph, and set it in front of me. "Take a minute," he said.

"I keep telling you," I said, "I don't know anything about that key. I've never seen it before."

He shrugged, put it back in the bag, wrote something on the outside of the bag, then sealed it with a colored sticker. "The painting's not going to be much help," the chief said.

"Are you *kidding*? It's totally a crucial clue!" I said. "Mom was out there in forty-degree weather wearing nothing but a thin dress and carrying a watercolor painting. It's obvious she didn't intend to stay out there for long. Most likely she was giving this picture to somebody. If we could figure out what the painting was, why it was significant—hey, we might be able to figure out who killed her."

The chief said nothing as he took out another, larger bag. He broke the seal on the bag, pulled out a piece of paper. I recognized it as expensive watercolor paper. He handed it to me.

I turned it over, frowned. The paper was a pale feature-less white, barely tinged pink here, yellow there.

"That's not it," I said. "Look at the photograph. It's a totally different picture."

"Uh . . ." the chief said. "I'm afraid what happened is that the crime scene was secured and then the temperature rose quickly. All that ice that had formed on the picture? It melted and washed away everything that was there."

"Who was the genius who let that happen?" I said sarcastically.

"That would be me," he said. "I had a lot of things to juggle. Securing the scene, taking photographs and measurements. It didn't even occur to me that a piece of evidence might be disappearing right under my nose. But the fact is, by the time I was able to look at it with any care, there was nothing left to see."

I held up the paper. I remembered my mom showing me one time how all fancy art papers have watermarks on them that tell you the brand name of the people that made the paper. I held it up to the light. The word REMBRANDT was imprinted into the paper. That was the kind my mom used.

"Frankly," the chief said, "we don't even know who painted it or what it looked like. It's pretty much useless."

I put the paper up close to my face and stared at the bottom left-hand corner. Handwritten in tiny letters it said:

KBC—7/7/05—29.71

"What?" the chief said.

"That's her signature," I said.

He took the paper from me and stared at it. "You're sure?"

I nodded. "KBC, that's her initials. That's the date she painted it, 7/7/05. Two days before she died."

"And these other two numbers?"

"She numbered every single painting or drawing that she did," I said. "She was always working on, like, a series or whatever. You know, a bunch of pictures in the same style or something? So this was the seventy-first painting in the twenty-ninth series."

"Hm." The chief didn't seem interested in the painting. He kept fiddling with the bag that had the odd little key in it.

"What I'm saying is that if you could find the ones numbered, say, 29.70 and 29.72, and they were pictures of the same person, you could guess that 29.71 was a picture of the same guy. It might be the killer!"

The chief sighed loudly. Honestly, he seemed kind of tired and bummed out. And not very interested in what I had to say.

"Can I see the rest of the stuff?" I said. "Please, if I could see what you have, maybe it would help me to—"

He held up his hand. "Look, you seem like a good kid," he said. "I'm sorry as heck about what happened to your mom. And I feel terrible that I never solved the case. You deserve to know who did it. To have justice. But I can't let you see this." He sighed again. Then suddenly he stood up and got all busy and important-looking. "Look, I'm sorry, but I've got a lot to do today. . . ."

"What, you got a parking ticket quota to fill?" I said. "Or maybe you need to chase some ducks out of old Mr. Eastman's yard again?"

He gave me a hard look.

"I can help you, Chief Dowd," I said. "I can find out stuff. But not if you keep treating me like a moron."

Except I pronounced it *moe*-ron. Which was kinda weird.

10

I rode back out toward the school.

As I was passing the trailer park where the Jackstaff clan lived, I started getting this weird feeling. Without really making a decision, I turned off onto the gravel road and pulled my bike up in front of the trailer where my old friend Leo Jackstaff lived. It was a ratty, dented mobile home, with rust stains running down the side like the tracks of red tears. All kinds of junk lay around in the dirt.

A large, lean dog with some kind of skin problem that had made most of its fur fall off was chained up outside the trailer. It started barking and jerking on the chain as soon as I rode by, throwing itself at me.

After a minute a tall thin kid about my age, with a shock of bright blond hair, poked his head out the door. "Shut up, you stupid-ass dog!" he shouted. Then he spotted me. He looked me up and down with disdain. My green shirt and khaki pants made it obvious I was from The Arsenal. All the townies hated us. But the Jackstaffs had always been particularly fond of abusing Arsenal kids. "Kind of in the wrong neighborhood, ain't you?"

"Leo?" I said.

His eyes narrowed. Suddenly his eyes widened. "Davy? That you? Holy crap, I didn't even recognize you!"

"Can I talk to you for a minute?"

"Dude! Come on in!"

He threw open the door to the trailer.

The dog kept barking at me. "Don't worry about Racer," he said to me. "She don't bite."

Just to be sure, I circled around the dog, parked my bike, followed him inside. Sitting on the couch was a hulking guy with a scar on his left cheek. He was cleaning a pistol. He didn't look up when I came in. There was a big gun rack behind him, several hunting rifles, a shotgun, a couple of military-looking rifles. I noticed there was a black-powder rifle, too.

"Nolan!" Leo said. "You remember Davy? Davy Crandall?"

Leo was a lot different from the way he'd looked when I was a kid. But Nolan? Nolan was completely unrecognizable. The last time I'd seen him, Nolan had been a skinny guy of about eighteen with the same color blond hair as Leo. Now his head was shaved, and his arms were crawling with big muscles. Tribal tattoos wound around his neck, curling up onto the lower part of his jaw.

Nolan looked up at me at with cold eyes. I felt a shiver run through me. Then he went back to cleaning the gun.

"Don't mind Nolan," Leo said. "He just got out of the joint, so his social skills are little out of whack. They gave him a year in prison for poaching. You believe that? *Poaching?*" He laughed. "Of course it was his third offense."

I wasn't even totally sure what poaching was. Something to do with shooting deer at the wrong time of year, I guess.

"So what's up, dude?" Leo said. "You want something to drink?"

"I'm okay." I sat on the chair opposite Nolan. "So look . . ." I said. "I actually had some questions for you. For both of you."

Suddenly the temperature in the room seemed to drop a little.

Nolan snapped the gun back together, sighted it at my head. It's basic gun safety that you never ever ever point a gun at a person. Not unless you mean to shoot them. So it kind of creeped me out. I knew the gun wasn't loaded—or at least I was pretty sure. . . .

"Oh," Leo said. "So it's not like you just dropped by to chill a little, shoot the breeze about the good old days?"

I shifted uneasily in my seat. Nolan was still pointing the gun at my head. "I don't suppose you'd mind pointing that at something else?" I said.

For a minute Nolan didn't move. "Pow," he said finally, his voice almost a whisper. I had forgotten the way he talked. Quiet, never raising his voice. He lowered the gun, pulled out the clip, and started filling it with bullets.

"Look, I just found out you guys were the ones who found my mom," I said. "I never even knew that before."

There was a long silence.

"Hey," Leo said finally. "I'm really sorry about your mom. That sucks. She was a cool lady."

I nodded.

"She was nice to me, you know?" Leo said. "When a lot of other kids' parents treated me like trash. Just because of my last name."

"I just wanted to know," I said. "I just wanted to know what you saw. What you found."

"Don't tell him nothing, Leo," Nolan said in his soft, menacing voice.

Leo looked at his brother nervously, then said to me, "Hey, it was dark. It was raining. We were just messing around out in the Barrens and there she was. We pretty much just ran off. I called the police. . . ." He shrugged. "Nothing more to it than that."

"Why are you telling him this?" Nolan said.

"This is my *friend*!" Leo said hotly, pointing at me.

Nolan snorted. "No, he's not."

"There's not much to tell," Leo said.

"You're an idiot, Leo," Nolan said. Then he stood up, shoved the pistol down in his pants, and walked out the front door.

"Jerk," Leo said, after he was gone. There was a loud rumble as a car cranked up, then roared away. Rocks, thrown up by the tires, clattered against the side of the mobile home. "Dude, can you believe that?" Leo gestured at the door. "He gets home from the joint, he takes my car anytime he wants. Like he owns it!"

"Why don't you just tell him not to?"

"Do *you* want to tell him not to?"

I laughed. "Not really."

Leo laughed, too. "Man, it's so cool to see you again," he said. His smile slowly faded. "Things were never quite the same after you went off to The Assenal." All the townies pronounced it "the *Ass*-uh-nal." It was partly the Down East accent, dropping the R sounds. But they gave it this extra little twist, emphasizing the *ass* part, just so you wouldn't forget how much they hated you.

"Yeah?" I said.

"You know how it is," he said. Then he shrugged, his face blank.

"Is there anything else you can tell me? Just tell me what you saw."

Leo stood up, got an energy drink out of the refrigerator. A moldly, musty smell hung in the air after he opened the fridge.

"Look," he said finally. "I just . . . don't remember that much. It was a while back."

"I don't know," I said. "If I'd found some dead lady? I bet I'd remember a good bit about it."

"You calling me a liar?" he said sharply.

I looked at him for a while, not breaking eye contact.

"Sorry," he said finally. "I just . . ." He sighed heavily, then drained most of his drink. "It was me and Nolan. We were just out goofing around in the Barrens. The security guys from The Arsenal patrol that part of the Barrens. God forbid a townie tread on the sacred property of The Arsenal! Anyway, point is, we had our flashlights off so they wouldn't spot us. I literally stumbled over her. After I tripped, though, I turned on my flashlight. Just to see what it was. I thought maybe it was a dead deer or something. But no. It's a lady."

He shook his head sadly.

"At first, I didn't even recognize her. I just saw this white dress, you know? With little blue dots. And this blood all over the front. Then I recognized her. I was like, 'Dude, that's Davy's mom.' Nolan didn't want to call the cops. We kinda argued. Finally I went back and called."

"How long before you called?"

Leo looked away nervously, then took a long sip on his drink. "Like . . . four, five hours?"

"Jesus, man!" I said.

He shrugged. "She was dead, dude. What good would it have done?"

"Yeah," I said.

"You know how Nolan is. He wants zero to do with cops. So he said he'd beat my ass. I had to sneak off after we got back just to make the call."

"Did you see anything while you were there?"

"Like what?"

"Clues?"

"Clues!" Leo laughed. "Dude, you been watching too much TV."

"Look, you know what I'm saying. Was there anything there that seemed weird? Anything lying on the ground? Footprints? I don't know—*anything*!"

"Your mom was lying there with a hole in her chest. Yeah, that seemed weird." Leo looked away from me. "Hey, I'm not trying to be a jerk. You know? I'm just saying, I didn't exactly sit around staring at her."

"Did you see the painting?"

"The what?"

"The painting. She had a painting with her. A little watercolor."

Leo frowned. "Gosh. Hm. No, I don't remember that." There was something funny about the expression on his face. I couldn't tell what it was, though. I wasn't sure if he was lying . . . or what.

"What?" I said.

"Huh?"

"You looked kind of . . . " I didn't finish the sentence.

After a second Leo's eyes narrowed. It had been a long time since I'd seen him last. We'd both changed a lot. I suddenly felt really distant from him. He scratched the tattoo on his arm, a picture of an ace of spades. "Dude, I don't know what you're talking about," he said.

"Did you see anybody while you were out there?"

He shook his head.

"There must be something," I said.

He threw his drink can in the trash, started rummaging around in the fridge.

"What about a key? Did you see this weird-looking little key lying next to her hand?"

He froze. Then he stood up. "I keep telling you," he said. "It was *dark*."

"Yeah, but . . ."

"Hey, look," he said. "Actually? I need to get to work."

"Oh, too bad," I said. "Where you working?"

He jerked his head in the direction of the village. "My cousin CJ's welding shop."

I'd never heard of a job that started at 3:30 in the afternoon. Plus, he didn't have a car to drive himself there. But I could see I'd gotten about everything I could out of him.

"You think of anything, give me a shout," I said.

"Yeah."

"Good seeing you, Leo."

"Yeah." He looked at me for a second, half sad and wistful, half resentful.

I went outside, grabbed my bike, and rode away fast—the dog barking and barking and barking, hurling itself at the end of its chain until I disappeared over the hill.

Back at The Arsenal, as I crossed campus on my bike, I spotted Misty Cleary. I don't really know why, but just seeing her made me feel all flustered. I steered out of my way, rode toward her. I didn't really have anything to say to her, though, so I just rode my bike right by her.

"Hi, Misty," I said.

She just kept walking, didn't even look at me. I turned around. Swish, swish, swish. She didn't even break stride.

Then there was this huge noise and everything went black.

When I woke up, Garrett Rothenberg was staring down at me. "You okay, Worm?" he said.

"What happened?"

"You were staring at Mindy and you ran into the Dumpster behind Gifford House."

"Oh, crap," I said. I sat up slowly. My head was killing me and my bike was totally trashed.

"See?" Garrett pointed at the side of the green steel trash bin. "That dent's where your head hit."

I groaned.

"Look, get real," Garrett said. "A chick like that? One, she's out of your league. Two, if you were lucky enough to get with her for ten seconds, she'd just stomp all over your heart and wreck your life."

"I don't know what you're talking about."

"Plus, three, I got first dibs on her." He stared at me for a second, then held up his hand, two fingers extended. "How many fingers?"

"Two."

"Close enough. You're fine." Then he turned around and walked off in the same direction as Misty had gone.

I stood up and carried my wrecked bike across the quad, everybody laughing at me, feeling like the biggest dork in history.

I waited until supper time to sneak into my house. *(Thank you, Dad, for taking away Main Meal today!)* The only good news about missing Main Meal was that everybody else in the school was in the dining hall, so I'd be able to sneak into the house without being detected.

And why, you may well ask, would I have to sneak into my own house?

Because, of course, my dad wouldn't want me to get special treatment. God forbid I get to sleep in my own bed occasionally, or grab a snack from the freezer, or in any way live a normal life. No, that would smack of favoritism. I lived in the dorm—just like all the other kids. Period.

Well, in theory, anyway.

But what kind of moron—*okay, I'm gonna have to stop using that word*—wouldn't be able to figure out a way to get into their own house? Key under the doormat, climbing the drainpipe, whatever. In my case, it was the broken latch on the downstairs bathroom window.

Easy as pie, I was inside.

First, I grabbed a quick sandwich. Then I went upstairs to my mom's studio. After Mom died, Dad had closed the door to the studio where she painted—and as far as I knew, he'd never gone back in. (Which I thought was a little weird. But, hey, it's his life.)

Anyway, I pushed open the door and went in. The room was large and bare, with two big windows along one wall, canvases stacked against the other. An easel was still set up at the near end of the room, a palette sitting on a small table next to it, dried-up oil paints still sitting there waiting to be used. The canvas had been painted white, and then a human figure blocked out with tan paint. But there was no face on the figure, no definition to the limbs or torso, nothing beyond a featureless blob. You couldn't even tell if it was a man or a woman she'd been starting to paint.

It was as though someone had interrupted her in mid-brushstroke.

At the far end of the room was a seat where whoever was modeling for her must have been sitting.

All kinds of memories came flooding back. I could still remember the exact smell of the room. Turpentine, linseed oil, glue . . . Even two years later, the smell still hung in the air. It was the exact smell of my mother. Some people's moms smell like perfume, some like apple pie, some like hair spray. But my mom smelled like paint.

I hadn't been in the room in a long time. It hit me like . . . well, not quite like a bullet in the chest, I guess. But it made me feel really strange and sad.

At the far end of the room was a walk-in closet where Mom kept all her old paintings. I walked into the dark little space, reached up, and pulled the chain that turned on the forty-watt lightbulb hanging from the ceiling.

I blinked. Last time I'd come in here, there had been rows and rows of drawings and sketchbooks and paintings stacked or leaned next to one another in shelves along both walls.

But now there was nothing. It was dead empty.

I couldn't believe it. Dad must have done something with them.

My heart sank. My plan had been to come back, locate the watercolor series she had been doing, and find series 29, paintings 70 and 72. Like I'd told the chief, they probably showed who she'd been painting on those last few days of her life. And the painting they'd found lying next to her?—

hey, it could be the killer. Why not, right? At least it would be a start.

But now that was impossible. Her whole life's work was gone.

Just as I was about to hurry back out of the house, I heard a noise from downstairs—the sound of the front door being opened.

I didn't move. What next? If I just sat there for a while, I'd be okay. Dad usually did some paperwork in his office after dinner, so I'd just sneak out after that.

Then I remembered that I had left the bag of potato chips and the remains of the sandwich out on the kitchen table. Stupid!

"David!" It was my dad, yelling at the top of his lungs. "David! Where are you?"

I didn't move. I heard his footsteps clumping up the stairs. They stopped in front of the door to the studio. Which, I also remembered, I hadn't closed.

"David!" Dad didn't walk into the studio. He just stood there, looking through the open door. "David! Get out here this minute!"

I felt my heart sink. I slouched out into the hallway.

Dad was standing there shaking his head. "Do you realize how this makes me feel?" he said. "When I assign you to miss Main Meal or take a cold shower, it's not just a punishment to you. It's—"

I had heard the lecture about a million times and didn't

need to hear it a million and one. "I didn't come here to eat," I interrupted.

He blinked, looked at me in disbelief. "Are you telling me that plate with all the sandwich crumbs on it just *walked* into the kitchen?"

"No, that's not what I'm saying. I came here to find one of Mom's paintings."

"Oh!" he said. "And it was just a matter of convenience that you were able to steal a sandwich while you were at it."

"Steal? This is *my* house!"

"Not during the school year. You know this."

"Dad, I'm just trying to find . . ." I gestured at the studio. "What happened to all Mom's stuff?"

"Don't change the subject, young man."

"Dad! I just wanted to look at her paintings! What did you do with them?"

"Her paintings were mine to dispose of as I felt necessary. I disposed of them."

I felt a sudden wave of anger wash over me, so strong I almost felt sick. "*Your* paintings? What about me? She was my mom! You didn't even ask me if I wanted them."

"We're discussing your sandwich. Not your mother's hobby."

"Hobby? This was a little more than a hobby, wouldn't you say?"

"How did you get into the house?"

"Why do you even care?"

"How did you get into the house?"

"Through the damn bathroom window, how do you think?"

My dad slapped me in the side of the head. It hurt a little. But mostly I just felt humiliated and angry. "Young man," he said. "I'm terribly, terribly disappointed in you. I'm not even going to punish you. I can see punishment has no effect on you."

"Whatever."

"But hear this, young man: If I have to punish you one more time this year—you're off the rifle team."

"You're such a jerk," I said. "I wish Mom had shot you. Instead of the other way around."

Dad stared at me. "Ex*cuse* me?"

I pushed past him, walked down the stairs. I could feel tears stinging my eyes now, and my blood was thundering in my ears.

"One more mistake!" Dad called. "*One* more, and you're off the team."

And that was about it for my big investigation. I asked around, but nobody seemed to know anything about the key or about who Mom had been painting there at the end or who might have had a grudge against her. I prodded Mr. Entwhistle, but he seemed to have said all he had to say on the subject of my mother. I talked to a couple of people who'd worked with her, but they had nothing useful to add. Bottom line, I got nowhere.

The school year went on. I made mediocre grades, I kept my head down, and I practiced shooting with Misty Cleary. My shooting just got worse and worse. I don't even know why I kept working with her. All she did was abuse me. For a while I even thought she was intentionally screwing me up. Maybe to torture me. Maybe to make sure she won First Shot.

But eventually I came to realize that she couldn't have cared less about First Shot. She had her sights on bigger things. Occasionally she'd disappear for a weekend, then come back and not say where she'd gone. But the word got out in school that she was winning shooting trophies at these big matches all over the country.

I kept shooting and shooting and shooting, getting worse and worse and worse. So, why did I keep coming back? Maybe because Misty was so beautiful. But she wasn't just beautiful. After a while you started to see she was a lot more interesting than she let on. She was really smart and had read a lot of weird books that you wouldn't think some cute girl from Mississippi would read.

But she never really let you in. So you were always guessing about her.

And Garrett Rothenberg had been right in his obnoxious predictions. They started going out with each other about a month into the first semester of school.

Garrett was always sneaking out with her, and then eventually he'd come back and tell me all these stories about stuff they'd done. I suspected it was all lies. I *hoped* it was lies. But with Garrett, you never knew. Then she and Garrett would have a big fight and they'd shout at each other, then they'd break up and I would feel good for a few days. And then the next thing you know, you'd see them walking hand in hand together on the quad.

Then something odd happened. During the late spring— about a month before graduation—my shooting suddenly started getting dramatically better. Not better than Misty— in fact, not even as good as my shooting had been before

Misty started shooting with me. But better. Suddenly I stopped shooting sixes and sevens. It was mostly eights and nines, with the occasional bull's-eye. I was starting to get the hang of all the technical stuff she'd been teaching me. I could feel it coming. Everything she'd been teaching me was starting to settle into my bones.

Week by week, day by day, shot by shot, I was getting better. At first I thought it was my imagination. But then it was too obvious.

I finally knew for sure that things had turned around when—three days before the shoot-out that would determine who made First Shot—I fired ten shots while Misty watched through the spotting scope. When I was done she just said one word to me. "Damn."

Nothing else. Not, "Nice shot." Not, "Hey, good job." Not, "You're really coming along, Worm." Just that one word: "Damn."

My heart about cut a backflip.

And then, five minutes later, everything changed.

13

The phone rang on my hallway as I was putting up my rifle. Nobody's allowed to have cell phones at The Arsenal, and the only phones we have are sitting out in the middle of each hallway in the dorm, bolted to the wall.

"Worm!" somebody shouted. "Yo, Worm! Phone!"

I went out and answered it. I never got phone calls. Never. "Hello?" I said.

"Davy?"

It took me a second. "*Leo?*"

"Davy. I need your help."

"My help? For what?"

"Just—look, can you come out to my place?"

It wasn't a good time. We had finals coming up and I was in bad shape in a couple of classes. "Well . . ."

Then the phone cut off.

For a second I thought he'd hung up on me and I decided, hey, the heck with him, I'd just go to the library and get some studying done. But I kept thinking about the sound of his voice. He sounded really scared. And suddenly I wasn't sure he'd hung up on me at all. It was like somebody had cut the line.

I carried my bike downstairs and started riding.

My bike had never been the same after I ran into the Dumpster. The front fork was a little bent, the rear brakes squeaked, and the front tire was just slightly out of round, so that the whole bike vibrated as soon as you got over about five miles an hour.

But it was all I had.

I arrived at Leo's place ten minutes later, my hands buzzing slightly from all the vibration in the handlebars.

Leo's car was gone, but his dog was still there. The dog threw itself at me, same as it had last time. I got off the bike and banged on the front door of his mom's trailer. The dog was chained up so that it got within about a foot of the door. It was yanking and slamming against the chain, teeth bared. I just hoped the chain would hold.

After a minute the door opened and Leo's mom looked out at me. She was a very thin, nervous-looking woman who always had a cigarette in her mouth. I hadn't seen her in a long time. She looked a lot older to me now, her skin lined and hardened; her once-blonde hair had gone thin and white.

"Shut up, Racer!" she screamed, her cigarette dribbling ashes on her shirt. The dog ignored her. Then she looked at me irritably. "What," she said.

"I don't know if you remember me," I said. "David Crandall? I use to be—"

A large smile broke out on her face, revealing stained teeth. "Davy! Well, look at you!"

"Leo just called me," I said. "Is he here?"

"Leo?" she said. Her smile faded. "Him and Nolan moved out about six months ago." She gestured with her thumb toward the rear of the trailer park. "They got a little trailer back there."

"Okay," I said. "I better go see what he needs."

The mention of Leo seemed to have extinguished Mrs. Jackstaff's brief pleasure at seeing me. She nodded silently and closed the door.

I started walking back through the trailer park. Various members of the Jackstaff clan were sitting outside their trailers. It was a hot day for Maine this time of year, close to ninety degrees, and the trailers must have been stifling. Practically every Jackstaff in the town was sitting outside their trailers, silently drinking beer and smoking. They watched me walk through the knot of trailers without speaking, their eyes sullen and resentful. They were a sad, tough-looking bunch. Men with ponytails and beards and missing fingers. Women with bad skin and missing teeth. Dirty little shoeless children.

My heart was thumping away in my chest. I felt like I was in a zombie movie or something, the only normal person left, while all these freaks were staring at me, waiting to do something terrible to me.

I nodded and smiled at one old guy with a gold tooth and a ruined milk-white eye that stared off at a strange angle. He just looked at me with his one good eye, then spit on the ground.

Okey-dokey, I thought. *I get the picture.*

I walked among them until I reached the far end of the trailer park, then looked around. No sign of Leo.

"Anybody know where Leo is?" I said.

Blank stares.

"Leo Jackstaff," I said. "I'm looking for Leo."

I heard the sound of a beer can being popped open. Otherwise, silence.

"He called me. . . ." I said.

Nothing moved. And then, finally, a little kid—maybe five years old, shirtless, legs dirty, face smeared with some brown food—raised one stained hand and pointed.

At first I didn't see it. It looked like the kid was just pointing at a bunch of ratty bushes and trees. But then I saw the nearly invisible footpath, just a dirt trail no more than a foot wide where the weeds had been trampled down. It led off into the trees.

I followed the path back through the trees, feeling the eyes of the entire Jackstaff clan boring into my back. The farther I walked, the more nervous I felt. The trees abruptly grew together, blotting out the late-afternoon light. I thought my heart was going to beat out of my chest.

But then, after walking for a minute or two, I finally

came out into a clearing. A tiny, miserable trailer—the kind you towed behind a car—sat in the middle. Around the trailer lay a litter of junk. Old cars, a refrigerator, a couple of stoves, lots of other stuff—all of it rusty and overgrown with creepers and briars.

I walked to the trailer and banged on the door.

After a minute the door opened. Leo looked out at me. He seemed thinner than the last time I'd seen him. He smiled. "I thought you wouldn't come," he said.

"The phone got cut off," I said.

"Oh." He motioned me inside. I entered and found myself inside a tiny room. Everything was neat and shipshape. But there was a bad smell in the place, like a dead animal. To my right was a tiny kitchenette—just a hot plate and counter, really. To my left were two beds. Books were stacked in neat rows, hundreds and hundreds of them, next to one of the beds.

On the bed near the books lay an old man.

Or that's what I thought at first. His cheeks were sunken, his arms thin, his head bald, his skin a strange grayish color. Then I saw the tattoo swirling around his neck and up onto his chin. It was Leo's brother, Nolan.

"Man!" I said. "What happened to him?"

"Cancer," Leo said.

"But he's only like twenty years old!"

Leo nodded. "The cancer he's got, it's treatable. But he won't go to the doctor."

"Who's been taking care of him?"

Leo shrugged. "Just me."

"So . . . what do you need me for?" I said.

"He's gotten so bad, he can't stop me from taking him to the hospital now. I need somebody to help me get him there."

"But . . ." I pointed in the direction of the trailer park.

He shook his head. "They won't help."

"Why not?"

Leo sighed. "Long story."

"Can't you call an ambulance?"

"I called them three times. They kept saying they were out on other calls. Last time an ambulance came out here, somebody beat up one of the ambulance drivers. The volunteer fire department guys pretty much made it known: if a Jackstaff gets hurt?—hey, pal, figure out your own way to get to the hospital."

"What about your car?"

"I sold it to get medicine for him."

"I'll call Dad," I said. "He'll know what to do."

Leo handed me his cell phone. I called Dad, explained the situation. Dad said he'd take care of everything.

We sat for a while on the bed opposite Nolan. Occasionally Nolan stirred. He seemed to be sleeping fitfully

"You know he made a perfect score on the SAT?" Leo said.

"You're kidding," I said.

Leo nodded. "He reads all the time. Not just like junky action books. Philosophy. Religion. Science. He talks to me every now and then and it's like . . ." He made a slicing motion over his head with his hand. "There's no telling what he could have done if he had set his mind to it." He shrugged. "But he's a Jackstaff, you know what I mean? He's doomed."

I looked at Leo. "Is that what you think?" I said. "You're doomed?"

He laughed cynically. "Nobody named Jackstaff has amounted to squat in two hundred years. What in the world makes you think that would change with me?"

"I don't know," I said.

Nolan stirred again. One eye opened. Then the other. They were the same cold blue that I remembered. It was the only thing about him that didn't look pretty much dead. He stared at me for a minute. Then one hand rose from the sheets. His finger twitched. He seemed to be beckoning to me.

I leaned forward tentatively.

His finger kept twitching. I put my ear close to his mouth. I could smell him now. It was Nolan that I'd smelled when I walked into the trailer, the smell of somebody dying. It was really sad and really repulsive at the same time.

He whispered something to me. It sounded like he was saying the letters "I. A."

"What?" I said.

"I . . . ain't . . ." He took a long, deep breath. *Not I. A.—I ain't . . .*

"What?"

"I . . . ain't . . . gonna . . . make it," he said. Then he took a long, slow breath.

"Sure you will," I said. I patted him on the arm. It was hard to believe that somebody who'd seemed so frightening just nine months ago now seemed so pathetic.

He gestured to me again.

"A . . . round." He took a deep breath. "Around . . . my . . . neck," he said. "Yours." Then he sank back onto the pillow.

I looked questioningly at Leo. Leo seemed uncomfortable. He wouldn't meet my gaze.

"What?" I said. "What's he talking about?"

"Around his neck," he said. "Go ahead. Take it."

It took me a moment to figure out what he was talking about. But then I saw that around his thin neck Nolan was wearing a cheap little chain—like a lightbulb pull chain.

"Yours . . ." Nolan whispered. "Take it. Tunnel." Then his eyes closed, and he sank back onto his pillow.

"Tunnel?" I said. "What do you mean?"

I reached out tentatively. His skin felt papery, like it might tear if you just touched it. I gently pulled the chain off of his neck. He didn't move at all.

And there, hanging from the chain, was a small steel

object, just slightly rusted. It was the perfect mate to the one that Chief Dowd had showed me.

A key.

I stared. Then someone was banging on the door.

It was my dad: "David?" he called. "David, are you in there? Come out here right this minute."

I stuffed the key quickly into my pocket.

14

Dad was pissed. I mean, seriously.

"What's the big deal?" I said after we'd delivered Leo and Nolan to the hospital.

"Look, I know you're trying to do a good thing. I know you used to be friends. But you can't help those people. Take it from me."

"What people?"

"The Jackstaffs."

"That seems a little harsh."

"Did you know that Nolan went to The Arsenal for two years?"

I shook my head.

"Scholarship student. Not a boarder, just came during the day and went home. Bit of an experiment, actually. Ultimately a failure. The third time he was caught stealing, we had to send him home for good."

"What did he steal?"

"Oh, he used to come in the middle of the night, break into the old buildings, sneak around in the tunnels."

"What tunnels?"

He looked at me curiously. "I guess you wouldn't know about them, would you? Well, as you know, the school was originally built here on top of a Revolutionary War fortification. It was an arsenal that held weapons and powder and so on for the local militia. Ultimately they tore down all the battlements to build the school buildings. But there were tunnels underneath the school—part of the old fortification—that were never destroyed." He cocked his head. "You sure you never heard about this?"

"Well . . . I guess I heard a few stories. But, you know, people say there's a ghost of some pirate ship captain out in the Barrens, too. Doesn't mean it's true."

"Well, in this case it *is* true. Back in the seventies a couple of kids snuck into the tunnels and got hurt. So your grandfather Boyce had them sealed shut back when he was headmaster. Somehow Nolan figured out how to get into them. Far as I know, he's the only person who ever did that. And he was able to use them to get up into Crandall House somehow. Climbed up and stole office equipment and that sort of thing. He was caught selling them at a pawnshop over in Dartington. We had to separate him from the school after that." Dad shook his head. "A shame, too. Very, very bright young man. But he had a screw loose. All the Jackstaffs do."

"Leo doesn't."

"Just because he seemed like a nice kid back when you were in fourth grade doesn't mean he's a nice guy now."

"Yeah but—"

"If he calls you again, you call me."

"But . . ."

"I don't want you to see him again. That's final."

"But—"

"You've got three days until the shoot-out for First Shot. I'm dead serious, son. If you see Leo Jackstaff again, you're off the Dartington Rifles. Period."

I fingered the strange key in my pocket. And wondered if there was something else going on here, some other reason Dad wanted me to stay away from Leo.

I felt something cold crawl up my spine. I shivered.

When I got back to the dorm, I put the key around my neck and hid it under my shirt.

15

The next morning I went out to shoot with Misty. She was fifteen minutes late—which was unusual for her—and her eyes were rimmed with red.

"You okay?" I said.

"I'm *fine*," she snapped.

"You and Garrett get into it again?"

"I said I'm *fine*."

"Okay," I said.

We didn't have to wear our neckties while doing athletics. Theoretically, shooting was an athletic endeavor, so I had taken my tie off. Which meant that when I leaned over to reload my rifle, the key swung out from inside my shirt. Before I could hide it, Misty's hand reached out and grabbed the key.

"What's that?" she demanded.

"Huh?"

"The key. Lemme see it."

"It's a key. Why would—"

She yanked on it.

"Hey, easy," I said. I pulled the key off, handed it to her.

She looked at it for a long time. "That's a very unusual key," she said.

"What, you're an expert?"

"My daddy collects locks," she said.

I looked at her for a second, trying to see if she was being serious. "Locks? That's a weird hobby."

She shrugged. "It's for a safe, right?" she said.

"I have no idea."

She looked at me like I was an idiot. "Then why are you wearing it around your neck?"

I didn't say anything.

She held it up near my face, pointed at it. There was some writing stamped into the metal. "See the markings? C & B Co. That's the maker. 2614, that's probably the serial number. It's unique to that key." She flipped it over. "Yeah, my guess is that it's for an old safe. This key is really carefully made. They wouldn't make a key this nice for an ordinary door lock. Probably a hundred, a hundred and fifty years old."

She handed it back to me.

"Look, why don't you e-mail me a picture of it? I'll send it to my dad. Maybe he can tell you more about it."

"Okay," I said. I didn't have a camera. But I knew where I could get my hands on one.

We set up at a hundred yards. Misty shot first while I

used the spotter scope. She hit nine tens in a row. The tenth shot was a little off, though, hitting the nine ring.

I loaded up and began shooting. Ten ring. Ten ring. Ten ring. Suddenly I felt this odd sensation.

Back when I'd first started really shooting well, probably in ninth grade, I used to have this feeling come over me—simultaneously calm and excited. It was like drinking liquid confidence. The feeling had faded over time. It wasn't that it went away, it just didn't seem quite as strong. And then, pretty much the minute I saw Misty shoot, it had disappeared entirely from my life.

Until this very moment. I kept shooting. Bang. Reload. Aim. Bang. Over and over. Ten ring. Ten ring. Ten ring.

Finally it came down to the tenth shot. I took a deep breath, settled the stock into my shoulder, let my heart rate steady. Wait . . . wait . . . wait. Squeeeeeeze. Bang!

Black-powder rifles produce a huge cloud of smoke. And sometimes you can't see your shot for several seconds. But I knew it had gone wide. I had felt a twitch, a tremor, just the tiniest interruption in the rhythm.

"Nine," she said.

I moved to the spotter scope. Misty didn't move. Like she was so shocked with my shooting that she was glued to the scope. I actually sort of had to nudge her with my shoulder to get her to move. And even then, she only moved just far enough for me to get my eye on the eyepiece. I could feel her shoulder against me, her hair brushing my skin.

It *was* a nine, just barely on the line between the eight ring and the nine ring.

"Good shooting," she said.

It was the first time I'd ever heard her compliment me.

"Not as good as you," I said. "That last shot was almost in the eight ring."

I could still feel her shoulder against me. This weird feeling of warmth and confidence and calm just *poured* through my veins. I mean, I know it was nothing. All I was doing was brushing up against her shoulder. But still, it felt like something to me.

"Seriously," she said, nudging me with her shoulder. "What's in it?"

"What's in what?"

She looked at me closely, an impatient frown on her face. She pointed at my chest. The key had escaped from my shirt again. "The safe, you dummy!"

"I don't even know if it's for a safe."

She studied my face. "Well, it must be *something* valuable," she said. "Only a *moe*-ron would wear a key around his neck that didn't open something valuable."

"I guess."

"So then where's the safe?"

"I have no idea," I said.

"Okay," she said. "Never mind. You *are* a moron."

Suddenly something struck me. "You know what?" I said. "Now that I think about it . . ."

16

After I put up my rifle, I went over and knocked on the door to my house. My *own* house, knocking on the door. Isn't that pathetic?

Dad opened the door and looked out at me. "Hello, Mr. Crandall," he said.

"Um, I needed some stuff from my room," I said. "Could I come in and get it?"

"What stuff?"

"A book. Doing a little extra credit project in, uh, history. I remembered I had a book upstairs that would help me."

He looked at me for a minute, then opened the door.

I ran upstairs, went into my room, got the copy of Caesar's *Conquest of Gaul* that Dad had given me for my birthday, then tiptoed into Mom's studio. Everything was covered in a heavy coating of dust. It still had that smell, turpentine and linseed oil. I felt a pang of emptiness remembering the way she used to smell.

But I wasn't there to torture myself. I had come for something. She had owned a digital camera. It was still sitting there, three years later, collecting dust. I picked it up and tucked it into my book bag.

"Thanks, Dad!" I called as I ran back down the stairs.

When I got back to the dorm, I pulled out the key, set it on the desk, and flipped on the camera. It did nothing.

For a second I thought it was broken. But then it occurred to me that the battery was probably dead.

"Hey, Rothenberg," I said. "You got any camera batteries?"

My roommate was getting all dressed up, putting on a suit. "Might," he said.

"What's with the monkey suit?" I said.

"Dad's up here for the big board meeting," he said. He never failed to remind you that his father was chairman of the board of directors of The Arsenal. "He's taking me out to dinner over in Portland. Gonna feed me a couple Scotches, tell me all his views on life. For the eightieth time."

I flipped the key over, looking at it again.

He looked over my shoulder, picked up the key. "What's this?"

"What's it look like?" I said. "It's a key."

"To what?"

"That's what I'm trying to find out. Misty's dad collects locks. She's gonna send a picture of it to him."

He dropped the key on the desk. "Don't even mention her name in my presence," he said.

"You guys break up again?"

"Had to ditch her, dude," he said. "She's cramping my style."

"I'm sure."

He pointed his finger at me. "Don't be getting the idea you can horn in on my action."

"What!"

"I see the way you look at her."

I made a big show of acting like he was nuts, rolling my eyes and stuff. "Anyway," I said, after I'd finished my little performance, "if you broke up with her, what do you care?"

He gave me a hard look, pointed at my face. "I got my eye on you, Worm."

"You ever heard of tunnels under the school?" I said.

"Everybody knows that's just a myth," he said.

I shook my head. "Nah, Dad says it's not. They closed them up a long time ago. But apparently there's a way in."

"Does that have something to do with this old key?"

"Maybe," I said.

He straightened his tie, opened the door to the room.

"Can you look for that battery real quick?" I said.

"Sorry," he said, not sounding sorry at all. "Gotta run, bro." He breezed out the door.

I waited until I heard him clomping down the stairs, then I opened the top drawer of his desk. I felt halfway bad about it. But I knew that he messed around with my stuff all the time. I can't count the number of times I'd seen him walking around campus wearing one of my shirts. He even wore my shoes sometimes. Needless to say he never asked. He'd just open up my stuff and start rummaging around. At the beginning of the year, I'd even caught him reading my e-mail. I actually had to change the password to keep him out of my computer!

So I figured, fair's fair, right? If he had a camera battery, tough luck, it was mine now. The top drawer of his desk contained a whole bunch of pencils, a copy of *Playboy*, a hip flask with some kind of liquid sloshing around in it, plus some rubber bands and a bunch of letters from his dad. But no camera batteries.

I took out his *Playboy* magazine, drew mustaches on all the naked girls, and put it back in his drawer. I pulled out the letters, looked at them for a moment. If I'd been a big snoop like Rothenberg, I'd have immediately ripped them open and read them. But I was more interested in finding a battery. I shoved them back into the drawer. As I did so, a package of batteries that had jammed in the drawer somehow came loose and fell down. I pulled a battery out of the package, shoved it into the camera.

After that, the camera came right on.

I took a couple of photos of the key, front and back, then uploaded them to my computer. They came out nice and clear, so I e-mailed copies of them to Misty.

• • •

After that I called Leo at the hospital. "So, how's Nolan doing?" I said.

"He's been in a coma since we brought him in. They said they've got to stabilize him before they can try chemo or anything like that."

"Oh, man . . ."

There was a long silence.

"So, look," I said. "Did Nolan ever say anything to you about some tunnels?"

There was a long pause.

"Leo?" I said. "Leo?"

17

Misty came over to me at Main Meal. Which is something she never, ever does. Outside of shooting, I don't think she's even said hi to me more than about five times this year.

She didn't say anything, just handed me an e-mail, then started to go back to the table with all the other cool girls from the senior class. I was just trying to make conversation, I guess, so I said, "Yeah, I'm gonna try and find the safe tonight."

She stopped, looked at me, shrugged. "So?"

"You ever heard of the tunnels?"

"What tunnels?"

"Under The Arsenal. I think that's where the safe is."

"I thought that was just a myth."

"Nah," I said. "The tunnels are real. It's just nobody knows how to get into them."

She raised one eyebrow. "Oh, but you do?"

I shrugged. "Wanna come?" I said. "Might be kinda cool."

She looked around like she was trying to see if anybody noticed her talking to a guy as insignificant as me.

"Midnight," I said. "Behind Crandall House."

She walked off without saying anything. I felt all disappointed. But who was I kidding, anyway? Misty wasn't gonna go crawling around in some tunnel with me. What was I even thinking? I stuffed the e-mail from her dad into my pants pocket.

At midnight I was lurking behind the back of Crandall House—a large gloomy structure in the middle of campus—waiting. The reason I was lurking was that if I got caught out there, I'd be in big trouble. Lights-out was at ten o'clock. Nobody was supposed to even be up reading after that—much less sneaking around campus.

I heard someone behind me clear their throat. I whirled.

It was Misty. She was wearing black pants and a black turtleneck, and had a black gym bag slung over one shoulder. Her face looked dramatic in the moonlight—like one of those movie stars from the forties. Suddenly I felt all sweaty and weird.

"So," she said. "Tunnels, huh?"

"Hey," I said. "You made it."

She shrugged. "I'm just bored."

"Cool." I tried to focus on not being a dork. This was the

first time I'd ever done anything with her other than blow holes in pieces of paper. "What's in the bag?" I said, pointing at the black bag slung over her shoulder.

"My burglary tools," she said.

"Okay, sorry I asked."

Misty looked around impatiently. "Well?" she said. "Where are they?"

"What?"

She looked at me like I was about the stupidest person she'd ever met. "The *tunnels*."

"Oh. Yeah. Well, I'm waiting for this other guy."

She cocked her head. "I thought you said you knew where they were."

"Well, I know a guy who knows where they are. It's pretty much . . . uh . . . the same thing." Okay, *total* dork.

Misty looked at her watch, sighed loudly.

Leo showed up about five minutes later. He was wearing a baseball cap and a T-shirt with the name of some heavy metal band I'd never heard of on it.

"Who's this?" he said sharply. "You didn't say you were bringing your girlfriend."

"She's not my girlfriend."

"Whatever, dude," he said.

"So how do we get into the tunnels?" I said.

"See, that's the problem," he said. "First, we gotta break into Crandall House."

"Oh, great," I said.

"Yeah. Then we gotta break into your dad's office."

I blinked. "How we gonna do that?"

He looked at me curiously. "He's your dad. I figured you could sneak his keys or something."

I looked at him with an expression that must have said, *I am a total helpless loser.* "Uh . . ." I said.

"You can't sneak into his bedroom, grab his keys?"

"Uh . . ."

Misty shook her head, looking disgusted. "Amateurs," she said.

"Oh, you got a solution?" I said hotly.

She unzipped the black bag that was hanging over her shoulder and held up this thing that looked like one of those hot glue guns they use in art class. Except it had this little probe thing sticking out of the end.

"What's that?" I said.

"A lock-picking gun, of course," she said.

I looked at Leo. Leo looked at me. A lock-picking gun? For a second I thought she was joking. But when she marched quickly up the stairs toward the front door, it finally occurred to me that she was being serious.

"Where'd you *find* this chick?" Leo whispered reverently.

"I'll unlock the door," she said. "You two make sure nobody's coming."

She clambered up the stairs to the rear entrance of Crandall House, stuck the probe into the lock, then pressed the trigger on the little gun. It emitted a harsh buzzing noise that lasted about ten seconds. When the noise stopped, she turned around and gave us a thumbs-up. Then she opened the door.

"Where *did* you find this chick?" Leo repeated.

"We practice shooting together."

"Shooting? Like . . . guns?" Leo clutched his chest. "Oh, that's just about the hottest thing I've ever heard in my life."

We ran up the stairs and into the building.

Misty was already halfway up the stairs. My dad's office was on the second floor.

"Hey, wait!" I called. "Where'd you get that thing from?"

"Dad gave it to me for my sixteenth birthday," she said. She had a very small but amazingly powerful little flashlight in her hand, pointing at the floor.

"Your *dad* gave you a lock pick for your sixteenth birthday?" I said. "What is he—a jewel thief?"

"No, he's an international security consultant. He's the one who taught me to shoot."

"He must be the world's coolest father," Leo said.

"Not really. He's just a boring little bald guy who happens to be into locks and guns."

"Black belt in Tae Kwon Do?" Leo said.

"Karate, actually." She was still marching up the stairs.

Leo and I tiptoed after her.

"Can he skydive?" Leo pursued.

She shrugged. "Well, yeah."

"He know how to fly an airplane?" I said.

"Mostly helicopters, I think."

Leo snickered. "Just a boring little bald guy, huh?"

When Misty reached the door that said E. J. CRANDALL, HEADMASTER on a brass plaque, she leaned over and looked at the lock. "Hm," she said.

"What's the problem?" I said.

She shined her powerful little flashlight on the lock. "Can't pick this with a lock pick," she said. "This is a Chubb 9000 series."

Leo and looked at each other. "Duh," I said. "It's a Chubb 9000 series."

"I knew that," Leo said.

It's weird, but even though we hadn't seen each other in years, it was suddenly like only ten minutes had passed. I just felt comfortable again, like I had my old friend back.

"So are we screwed?" I said.

"The only way to get into one of these is if you have a blank key that fits it."

"Gee," I said. "Don't happen to have one of those on me." I turned to Leo. "Leo?"

He made a big show of it, patting his pockets. "Gosh, no, left mine at home."

Misty smirked. "Fortunately, however . . . " She reached

into her bag, pulled out a giant ring of keys, and started trying to fit them into the lock. It took about five minutes, but
finally she got one to go.

Just as the key slid into the lock, a loud noise—*BOOOM*—
echoed through the old building.

"What the hell was *that*?" Leo whispered.

I shook my head.

We all froze. Misty clicked her light off. It was incredibly
dark suddenly, nothing but a few stray moonbeams coming
into the high old windows. As my eyes grew accustomed to
the dark, I began to see shapes around us. Shapes with eyes.
My heart was slamming in my chest.

It took me a second to realize that they were old oil
paintings, famous graduates of the school. Some of them
were my ancestors. The ones with the grimmest, gloomiest
eyes—they were guaranteed to be Crandalls.

We must have sat in the darkness for five minutes. Finally
Misty's light winked on. "I don't think anybody's down
there," she whispered.

"Maybe it was the pipes or something," I said.

"Well, it sure creeped *me* out," Leo said.

Misty took a small metal file out of her bag and started
filing on the key she'd put in the lock. "How long's this
gonna take?" Leo said.

"Five minutes? An hour? I don't know."

"Yeah, but—"

"The more you blabber, the longer it'll take," she whispered. "Hold my light."

I took the flashlight. It was small, black, heavy, with sharp little teeth sticking out around the part where the bulb was. I gathered the idea was that you could use it as a weapon as well as a flashlight. Misty worked intently—filing, putting the key in the lock, turning, taking it out, filing some more, sticking it back in, trying it. After a while sweat started building up on her upper lip. I don't know why, but it made her look even more beautiful.

Leo went to the bottom of the stairs and started wandering around the building. Suddenly he charged up the stairs. "There's somebody coming outside," he hissed. "I think it's the security guard."

"I've almost got it," Misty said.

"We gotta go," I said.

"I've almost *got* it." She kept filing.

Downstairs I heard something. Loud footsteps coming up to the front of the building. Then keys jingling. "Come *on*!" I said.

But Misty just kept filing.

Downstairs I heard a jingling noise, then a key sliding into the front door lock. It wasn't that big a building. If the night security guy came in, he'd hear us for sure. The front door creaked.

"Let's go!" I whispered, flicking off the flashlight. I

pointed to a cubbyhole down the hallway. If we all huddled in it, maybe he wouldn't see us. I pulled at Misty's shirt.

But she shook my hand off, lifted the key to the lock, slid it in.

The front door closed with an ominous thud. Footsteps headed across the lobby toward the staircase that led up to where we were sitting.

If we got caught up here, the security guard would go straight to Dad. And Dad had given me strict instructions: See Leo, you're off the rifle team.

"Let's *go!*" I hissed.

She twisted the key. It didn't move. She twisted harder. Still nothing.

The footsteps paused. The security guard was obviously standing at the bottom of the stairs. We all froze.

The footsteps began moving up the stairs.

Misty jiggled the key, still trying to turn it. I was making this goofy face at her, eyes bugging out, mouthing the words *Let's go let's go let's go let's go!* at her. But she wasn't paying any attention to me.

Suddenly, the key turned!

Misty rotated the key all the way. The lock emitted a soft click. It was hardly a noise at all. But in the quiet building, it seemed like a thunderclap.

"Hey!" a voice called. "Is there somebody up there?" The footsteps started moving faster now.

Misty flung open the door. The hinges creaked and we

practically flew through the door. I closed the door behind us as quietly as I could and twisted the lock. It all sounded incredibly loud.

We were now in the outer room of Dad's office, where his assistant sat.

"Hey!" the voice outside said. "Somebody in there?"

Then the doorknob shook. He was obviously trying to get in. There was a brief pause, then he shook the knob again.

"What the—" he said. I could imagine his puzzlement.

He gave it one more shake, then his footsteps started moving up and down the hallway. We sat in the dark, huddled together. I could feel Leo's elbow in my side, something soft in my back. It was some part of Misty's body. I could only imagine what it was.

"Hey!" the voice outside yelled. Then: "Oh, okay." Like he suddenly had figured out what the noises he'd been hearing were.

After that there was a strange snapping sound followed by a thud.

I looked at Leo. He seemed puzzled by the noise, too. But then the footsteps went back down the stairs and faded away.

"Whoa, that was close!" I said. "Nice work with the lock, Misty."

She shrugged and walked over to the door to Dad's inner office. She tried the same key in that lock. The door opened easily.

We walked in. During the day it was not exactly the brightest, most cheery room. But at night, it was downright creepy. There were more oil paintings of old guys on the walls, all of them looking down with disapproving gazes. One of them, a sour-looking old guy in a white powdered wig, leaned on a rifle.

"That's my great-great-great-great-something-or-other-grandfather," I said.

"Mean-looking old bastard," Misty said.

Leo walked over, grabbed the frame around the old guy's picture, and started yanking on it.

"Hey!" I said. "What are you doing?"

At which point he lifted the picture off the wall.

Behind the picture was a hole. A hole leading down into blackness.

Somewhere in the bowels of the building, we heard the noise again. *BOOOM!* It seemed like the sound was coming up out of the blackness.

"I don't know about this," Leo said.

"Hm," I said.

Misty started making a noise like a chicken, flapping her arms.

"Okay, okay, okay, okay," I said. "Let's go."

18

On the other side of the hole in the wall on my father's office was a set of steep wooden stairs. We walked slowly down them, trying not to make too much noise. A cool breeze blew upward, smelling of rocks and mold.

Eventually we found ourselves in a narrow tunnel, the walls of which were lined with rock. The mortar holding the rocks together was ancient and corroded, and in some places the walls bowed in like they were about to collapse.

"Cool!" Misty said. "So where's the safe?"

"Safe?" Leo said. "What safe?"

"That key your brother gave me," I said. "Misty says it's for a safe. And I think the safe is down here. I don't know where it is, but I think it has something to do with what happened to my mom."

At this Leo swallowed and looked kind of queasy.

"What?" I said.

He shook his head. "Well, let's find the safe."

We headed down the tunnel. Eventually it came out in a

small room with a conical ceiling. "There used to be a fort here," I said. "Back during the Revolutionary War. They tore it down eventually. But these little tunnels are underneath where the fort was."

"This was probably where they stored their powder and shot," Misty said.

Leo looked around. "I don't see a safe."

He was right. The room was pretty much empty. There was an old table and a chair with a broken leg over on the other side of the room, both covered with cobwebs. But nothing else.

BOOOOOM!

The sound echoed through the tunnel.

"What *is* that?" Leo said.

I shook my head. "Don't know. It's giving me the creeps, though."

We headed back up the tunnel, past the stairs leading up to Dad's office.

As it turned out, there was a maze of tunnels down there. And a lot of them didn't look that stable. I could see why they'd closed them up. If I'd been running a school, I wouldn't have wanted kinds sneaking around down there at night, either.

We went up one branch tunnel and down another, searching for the safe. But we didn't find it. In fact, we didn't find much of anything. Just tunnels and tiny rooms—some of them from the old fort, some of them probably basements for buildings that had been torn down long ago.

After a while I started feeling tired and frustrated.

"I don't know, guys," I said. "Maybe I guessed wrong. I thought for sure it was gonna be down here. But I think we've been in about every tunnel."

Misty shook her head. "Not all of them. Remember that one with the locked door?"

There had been a door. An old door, painted black, with an old-fashioned lock on it.

I shook my head. "Guys, I'm about gassed out."

Leo nodded.

Even Misty seemed tired. She looked at her watch. "Three-thirty," she said.

We all looked at one another. Simultaneously we all nodded.

BOOOOM!

"Plus, you know what?" Leo said. "I wouldn't mind if I never heard that noise again."

We laughed.

Suddenly Misty held her index finger up to her lip.

"What?"

"Shhh!"

We were all silent. Suddenly I could hear my heart beating.

I don't know how long we sat there. But it was a while. And then we heard it.

Crunch.

There was no mistaking it. It was a footstep. A furtive, sneaky footstep. Someone was following us.

Misty immediately turned out her flashlight. It got dark then. Dark like I'd never seen before in my life, a darkness so complete that the world seemed to simply go away. It was disorienting.

Crunch. Crunch. Crunch. The footsteps were getting closer and closer. My heart started beating faster.

"What are we gonna do?" I whispered.

Crunch. The footsteps stopped for a moment. *Crunch. Crunch.* They couldn't have been more than forty or fifty feet down the tunnel. So why was there no light?

I could almost feel Misty thinking, trying to figure out what to do. Whoever was down here, they needed light just as much as we did. Right?

Crunch. Crunch.

And then suddenly it was as though whoever it was had spotted us. But how could they? It was stone dark.

Suddenly Misty switched on her light.

And there he was. Looming over us, not more than thirty feet away—a tall man in a suit. His face was covered by a strange mask. It took me a moment to figure it out. It was one of those night-vision things, like soldiers wore so they could see in the dark.

In his hand was a gun.

Misty screamed.

"Run!" I shouted.

We tore down the tunnel, following Misty's light. She was a good athlete—but still . . . she was a girl, and she just couldn't run as fast as the guy behind us. I wanted to run faster, but I couldn't. Not without shoving her aside. The man behind us was gaining ground.

We twisted and turned through the maze of hallways. The guy behind us didn't say anything, didn't shoot—just followed. I couldn't really see him. The few times that I looked back, he was just a dark blur. I could hear him breathing, though.

"Hurry!" Leo shouted.

"Come on, speed it up!" I added. Over my shoulder I could see the mask flickering weirdly, like the face of a giant bug. He couldn't have been more than three or four strides behind me.

"I'm *trying*!" she yelled.

Then suddenly we passed through a door.

"Slam it!" Misty yelled.

I grabbed the heavy old door and heaved. It slammed into the masked man. I wasn't able to get it all the way closed.

"Help me!" I shouted.

All three of us leaned on the door. The man was really strong. He reached around the frame of the door. Misty pulled something out of her gym bag, slammed it into the man's hand.

There was a howl of pain and the hand disappeared.

It gave us enough of a break to close the door. There wasn't a lock. I looked around frantically for something to hold the door shut.

"Over there!" I yelled. An old wooden barrel stood by the wall. Leo grabbed it, started rolling it toward me. I struggled to hold the door shut while Misty and Leo jammed the barrel under the handle.

"That'll hold for about a minute," I said.

"Yeah, but where are we gonna go?" Leo said. "The only way back to your dad's office is through him."

The man started thumping against the door. The barrel shuddered.

"You think maybe he'll let us out?" Leo whispered.

"Hey, look," I yelled to the man. "I think there's some kind of misunderstanding here!"

The reply came in the form of a gunshot.

We were fifty yards down the tunnel by the time the echoes had died. "Okay, I think the answer to my question is no," Leo said.

"Where are we gonna go?" I said.

"The locked door," Misty shouted.

"Yeah, but it's *locked*," I said.

"So I'll pick the lock."

We ran down a long hallway and suddenly found ourselves face-to-face with the locked door. There was no other way out.

"Where's your lock pick?" Leo said frantically.

"Hold the light," Misty said.

I took the flashlight.

She took out a couple of small pieces of metal. "This should be easy," she said.

"You've done this before?"

There was a long pause. "Well. I've read about it in books."

"I hope you read carefully," Leo said. "'Cause it sounds like that dude's knocked the barrel out of the way."

"Light!" Misty hissed.

Looking back to see if the masked guy was coming, I had pointed the flashlight in the wrong direction.

"Sorry."

She slid two thin metal strips into the lock. One was straight, the other curved. She started jiggling them around. Sweat was pouring down her face now. I had neither the time nor the inclination to admire her. At that moment, mainly I just didn't want to die.

We could hear footsteps now. He was still a few hundred yards away.

"Hurry!" Leo said.

"You want to do it?" Misty said.

Give her credit, though. She didn't look frantic, didn't look scared. Her face was completely intent.

And it was at that exact second that I knew I was in love. All term I'd been dancing around it, trying to pretend like I wasn't completely gaga over this girl. And now, bang, I just knew.

"I'm in!" she said.

She yanked the door open.

The footsteps were getting closer and closer. Misty disappeared into the blackness. I followed.

And then, to my horror, I heard the sound of an impact, someone thundering into Leo. And then the door slammed shut.

"Leo!" I shouted. *"Leo!"*

There was only the sound of a scuffling.

"Go," Leo shouted. "I'll hold him off. Just go!"

Then the gun went off. *Pow!* The noise was incredible in the confined space of the tunnel. It was like being slapped in the side of the head.

"Go!"

"He's right," Misty said.

"Leo!" I shouted.

Pow! Pow!

"Leo!"

No answer. The man began thumping on the door. I noticed that there was a heavy bolt on the back of the door. It was an ancient iron thing, big around as my thumb. Misty reached for it.

"No!" I shouted.

"We can't do anything to help him now," she said urgently.

The door shuddered.

"Leo . . ." I said desperately.

Still there was no answer except for the thumping of the man's body against the door.

Misty shot the bolt. The end disappeared into the solid rock wall. "That'll hold him," she said grimly. She was right. That guy would never get through that door.

And neither would Leo.

"We gotta help Leo," I said.

She shook her head. "We can't," she said softly. There was a line of water running down from one of her eyes. I couldn't tell if it was sweat or tears. "We just can't."

Then she grabbed my hand and we started to run again.

We reached another door a few minutes later.

This one wasn't locked. We pushed through the door and found ourselves in a tiny room. It seemed much newer than the other rooms we'd been in. For a moment I wasn't sure why. Then I realized what it was: the walls weren't stone; they were concrete. At the far end of the room was a heavy steel door. With a modern lock on it.

"Hey, look!" I said. I walked over and tried the handle. It turned. But the door wouldn't move.

Misty ran her hand down the side of the door. "We'll never get out this way," she said.

"Why not?"

She shined her light on the edge of the door. Then I saw it: where the door met the frame, there was a globby-looking bead of metal. "It's welded shut," she said.

"Damn!" I looked around the room. Unlike the other rooms, this one was full of stuff. Ancient office furniture, old lamps, broken vases, horrible old landscape paintings . . .

"Oh my God!" Misty said.

"What." I didn't want any more bad news. I was still trying to process what had happened to Leo.

"Look."

Misty pointed her light. At the far end of the room was a black steel box about the size of a piano bench.

It was a safe.

I walked over to it, ran my hand down the face of the steel. The steel was cold and solid. At the top of the door on the front was a small brass plate embossed with the words:

CONSTANCE & BELL COMPANY

MODEL 9 SAFE

PAT. PENDING

PER. NO. 2614

I took the key from around my neck and looked to see where I should insert it. There were two small slots on the front of the safe. I wasn't sure which one to try. But I figured whichever one it fit into, that would be the one that worked.

"Yes!" I said. I slid my key into the lock and turned it. The key moved smoothly and certainly. There was no play in the lock. It felt tight and crisp as if it had been made yesterday. "Yes!" I said again.

Then I pulled the door. It didn't budge. My enthusiasm suddenly started to dim. Something was wrong!

I turned the key the other way, pulled again. Still nothing.

"Shoot," I said. "It's not working."

"Where's the other one?" Misty said.

"The other what?"

Misty stared at me. "You *did* read Dad's e-mail—didn't you?"

"Uh . . ." I said. "Not yet."

"Oh God," she said. Misty put her hands over her face.

I pulled the printout that she given me out of my pocket, unfolded it, and started to read her dad's e-mail.

"Don't bother." She snatched the note from my hand, wadded it up, and threw it on the floor. "His note said that it's a Constance & Bell patented double-lock safe. I think he said it was made in 1856. Your key has a tiny 'G' printed on the opposite side from the serial number. That stands for 'gate.' It opens the gatings in the mechanism. Then there's a second key. Almost identical to the one in your hand. Only it has a 'B' on the back. Which stands for 'bolt.'"

"No," I said.

"Without the bolt key *and* the gate key, you can't open the safe."

"No," I said. "Nooooo."

"You got your friend killed for nothing."

"We don't know he's dead," I said.

"Suit yourself," she said. Then suddenly her face softened. "I'm sorry," she said. "I shouldn't have said that."

Then she put her arms around my neck and hugged me, just about breaking my neck, she squeezed so hard.

I had the weirdest feeling for a second. It felt so good having her arms around me. After a minute her grip relaxed and then she kind of sagged against me. I could feel her hair on my face and my neck. I was flooded with a strange happiness. And for a second I felt like I would have sacrificed ten Leos for just one moment like that.

Then I just felt really horrible and scared.

I pushed her away. "Let's just go," I said gruffly. "There's got to be another way out."

And, in fact, there was.

It took us almost until daybreak to find it. But we finally did, walking down a nearly endless tunnel, the light in her flashlight getting slowly dimmer and dimmer and dimmer.

And then there it was. A tiny crevice in the rock, the thinnest, palest light coming in. It was barely wide enough for a human being to slither through. But we made it.

We crawled slowly, painfully through a jagged crack in the rock and finally emerged.

"Where are we?" Misty said.

Around us was a wild landscape of broken, twisted rock. I could hear the surf thundering below us.

"Jackstaff Tower," I said.

19

"**W**hat are we gonna do?" I said.

"Go shoot," Misty said. "Just like always."

We'd just snuck back onto campus, making it there at a little past six. The mist was rolling in off the ocean, wrapping the campus in thick fog. The old, dark buildings appeared and disappeared before us as the fog shifted.

"No, I mean about Leo," I said. "About that guy in the tunnels."

"Act normal. There's nothing we can do about it."

"We could call the police."

"And tell them what?—that some sinister guy in a night-vision mask was chasing us around in the tunnels in the middle of the night? They'll just go down there, find nothing, and then we'll get in a whole butt-load of trouble."

"Yeah, but what if Leo's still down there? What if he's hurt?"

Misty shook her head. "Don't be a *moe*-ron."

"What's that mean?"

She looked at me with her cool green eyes for a long time, her face expressionless. "Whoever was in that tunnel? Ten to one it's the same person who killed your mom. What happens if we go to them? They'll tell your dad everything we know."

I didn't say anything. On the way back from Jackstaff Tower I'd told her everything—about my mother's murder, about Dad burying something out by the tower, about the key that Nolan had given me, and its mate that was locked up in the evidence room at the Dartington Police Department.

"I still think we should tell the police."

"Are you insane?" she said. "Some guy just tried to kill you because you're trying to find out what happened to your mom. We've got to solve this ourselves. Fast. I mean, what if it *is* your dad? You're dead." She paused. "And probably so am I."

She had a point. "Yeah, but—"

"Look, Worm—"

"Could you just call me David?" I said.

She narrowed her eyes slightly. "Okay . . . *David*. Here's the thing. We'll get that other key, we'll come back tonight. Then we'll open the safe and find out what's going on. And if Leo's still down there . . . we'll do what needs to be done."

I looked around. The fog was so thick we might as well have been floating in space. You couldn't see anything at all.

"We don't have the other key," I said.

"So we'll get it."

"And how do you plan to do that?" I said.

"We better go get changed," she said. Then she disappeared into the fog. I felt for a moment like I was completely alone in the universe.

Then her voice floated out of the fog: "And all that hugging and holding hands and stuff? Heat of the moment. It never happened."

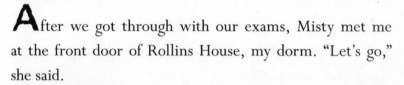

20

After we got through with our exams, Misty met me at the front door of Rollins House, my dorm. "Let's go," she said.

"Go where?"

She rolled her eyes. "Dude! To get the key."

"Yeah, but it's locked up in the—"

But she was already climbing on her bike.

We rode swiftly down Arsenal Road toward the village, past the trailer park where the Jackstaffs lived. I felt a jolt of nausea. The thought that Leo was probably dead because of me . . . Well, I couldn't even quite process it. I was almost numb. So I concentrated on keeping up with Misty, who was riding like she was in a race.

We pulled up in front of the city hall.

"What are we *doing*?" I said.

"Okay, here's the plan," she said. "This is a very small police department, right?"

"I guess."

"Okay, so the patrol guys are probably out on patrol. So that means the chief will be by himself."

"There's a clerk sometimes, too."

"Whatever. Point is, all we have to do is create a diversion. While they're distracted, I'll pick the lock on the evidence room, nab the key. Boom, we're golden."

"*We* have to create a diversion?"

"Technically? *You* have to create a diversion." She smiled.

I was still locking the bike as Misty headed for the door, swish, swish, swish. She had her black bag of burglary tools slung over her shoulder.

"Wait," I called after her. "What am I supposed to do? Set myself on fire?"

She got to the door. There was a sign on it that said, BACK IN FIVE MINUTES.

She tried the handle. It was locked. "Gee," she said, "good thing we don't have an emergency, huh?" She looked around furtively. "If you see anyone coming, yell."

"Wait a minute, wait a minute," I said. "There's got to be a better way of doing this."

But it was too late. By then she had her little automatic lock-picking gun in her hand. Breaking into a police station? What was she *thinking*?

Down the street I saw Chief Dowd. The way the building was constructed, you couldn't see the front door from the street. So Chief Dowd could see me, but he couldn't see

Misty. The chief was whistling as he walked, carrying a paper coffee cup and one of the famous elephant ear pastries that they served at the Five O'Clock Deli. He was about a block down the street, ambling slowly toward us. I estimated he'd be right in front of me within about half a minute.

I was so scared, I was pretty much looking for any excuse not to go forward with Misty's "plan." I mean, it didn't really seem like a plan at all to me. I don't know what the right word would be. Desperate move? Hail Mary pass? Dumb idea?

"Stop! The chief's coming!" I hissed.

But Misty kept attacking the lock with the pick gun. She seemed to be having trouble. "Not gonna work," she muttered finally.

"Thank *goodness*," I said.

But instead of walking away from the door, she just reached into her bag and took out some more tools—a tiny thing the size of a hairpin with a little hook on the end and a larger angled piece of steel. "Guess we're gonna have to do it the old-fashioned way," she said cheerfully.

She inserted the angled piece into the lock. It had a U-shaped gap in the steel that allowed her to stick the little hook into the lock after it. She raked the tiny pick delicately back and forth. "How much time have I got?" she said.

As Chief Dowd walked by Lincoln's Department Store, a woman with fake blonde hair came out, and they started talking.

"He's talking to somebody," I said.

Misty kept working on the lock. A couple of old ladies walked by. But I guess nobody would suspect that a girl in an Arsenal uniform would be trying to pick the lock on the front door of the police station in broad daylight. They didn't even give her a second look.

Chief Dowd tipped his hat at the lady with the fake-looking hair and started walking toward us. *Tipping your hat,* I thought vaguely. *Man, that's old school! Chief Dowd must be the last hat-tipper on the planet.*

And then, with a clank of the little cow bell hanging from the door, Misty was inside.

"Well, well," a voice said.

I looked up.

Chief Dowd was standing over me, blocking the sunlight. "Something on your mind, son?"

I could still see Misty inside the police station. She was motioning frantically at me, then pointed at the chief. She was mouthing some words to me. I couldn't tell what she was saying. But I could guess. She telling me to "create a diversion." Great.

I stared blankly at Chief Dowd. Create a diversion. What did that even *mean*? My heart was beating so hard I thought it might pop out of my chest.

"Son?" Chief Dowd said, frowning at me.

"Uh . . . " I cleared my throat. "No. I, uh, just . . ." And that was pretty much the extent of my diversion.

"You sure you don't have something you want to tell me?"

I shook my head. I imagine I looked like a total idiot. I felt like one, too.

"Okay, then," the chief said. He pulled a jingling set of keys off his belt and headed toward the door.

"Wait!" I called.

He stopped, gave me a hard look. "Son, if you got something to say, you need to say it. This is a serious business."

"I know," I said. "I know."

He kept looking at me impatiently. "*Well?*" he said finally.

"I . . . uh . . ."

I glanced over his shoulder. I realized that the police station was so small, you could actually see the door to the evidence room through the glass at the front of the station. If you weren't looking for her, you wouldn't notice. But the second the chief got to the door, there'd be no way he could miss her. Where he was standing, the chief's back was to her.

He took a bite of his elephant ear. "Son, why don't you come inside, sit down, make yourself comfortable. Then whatever you got on your mind, you just say it. Okay?"

I ran my hands across my face. Not only was I was coming across like a moron . . . but a *shifty* moron at that. "Um. Okay. Okay. Yeah, actually . . . okay, maybe I do have something to tell you."

Misty was still barely visible back inside the station.

"Could you, uh . . ." I was thinking desperately, trying to think of something to hold him up. "I need to lock up my bicycle."

"Okay, well, when you do, you just come inside and talk to me." The chief looked like he'd about had it. He turned toward the door.

"Wait!"

He stopped, sighed, looked back at me.

"The murder weapon!" I said. "I think I know where it is!"

He raised one eyebrow, tossed the elephant ear in the trash, wiped his hands on his pants, grabbed me by the elbow, and said, "Inside, young man."

By the time we got to the door, Misty was gone.

Where was she? Had she gotten into the evidence room? Was she hiding in the bathroom? I had no idea.

I felt dizzy and faint. What if Misty got caught? What if she got me in trouble? What if . . .

And then it hit me, what I'd actually said—in the grand scheme of things, getting in trouble was nothing. I had just told the chief that I had evidence of a murder.

The chief propelled me to the door, unlocked it, then pushed me through the lobby and into his office. Misty was nowhere to be seen.

I sat down in the chief's office. Chief Dowd perched on his butt cheek on the edge of his desk and looked at me for what seemed like about a year. Finally he said, "Talk to me, son."

I stood up, made a move to close the door.

"Leave it," he said. "It's fine."

But it wasn't fine. I didn't want him hearing Misty out there. I closed the door anyway.

Then I sat down again, put my face in my hands. Partly I was stalling for time. But partly I was trying to straighten some things out in my mind. I'd had this thought running around in my brain for close to a year now—but I'd never quite spoken it out loud.

"What if my dad did it?" I said finally.

He kind of chewed on the edge of his mustache for a second. He seemed a little sad—but also determined. "You think your father killed your mother," he said. "That's what you're telling me?"

Finally I said, "You remember back at the beginning of the year? You came by and asked to search the house? And Dad wouldn't let you?"

He nodded.

"Well, that night he went out and buried something over near Jackstaff Tower."

"How do you know this?"

"I followed him."

Chief Dowd ran his fingers through his ragged mustache. "And what did he bury out there?"

"I don't know." I shook my head, hesitated. "He had it

· 149 ·

wrapped up in a piece of plastic. But it looked like a rifle."

"And the reason you waited nine months to tell me this?"

I just looked at him.

"I know, I know," he said "He's your father. If I thought my dad had done something like that . . ." He didn't finish the sentence. Then he rapped his knuckles decisively on the side of the desk. "Well, okay. Look, son, I'm gonna need you to sign a statement. Write it all down. Then we're gonna get a warrant, go dig it up. Are you willing to help us do that?"

"Yes, sir."

The room was silent for a long time.

Suddenly the door to his office banged open. It was Misty.

"Oh!" she said. "There you are!" Her voice sounded oddly giddy. Misty was not the giddy type. It seemed like she was playing a role so the chief wouldn't take her seriously.

Chief Dowd glowered at her.

"I found that thing, David," she said. "You know, the thing we were looking for?"

"Uh . . ." I said.

"Young lady," Chief Dowd said. "We're in the middle of something very serious. I'd appreciate it if you'd go sit down in the waiting room."

"Oh! Gosh!" she said. "My bad!" Then she disappeared.

The chief took out a fresh pad of paper from a bookshelf

next to his desk. Then he handed it to me and said, "Write it all down."

I wrote until I got a cramp in my hand.

"I guess that's it," I said.

"Sign it and date it," he said.

I did.

"Now let's go do some digging," he said.

"Um, my friend and I were getting ready to . . ." My voice trailed off as the chief stared at me like I was losing my mind. "Sorry," I said.

The chief marched me out the door. Misty was sitting in the waiting room. I paused and said, "I'll see you back at school."

An hour later Chief Dowd and I—plus one of his officers— were out at Jackstaff Tower. Apparently everybody in town must have played out here when they were kids, because the chief and his officer argued the whole way about which was the best route out to the tower. The different routes even had names.

According to the officer, a chatty young guy with a blond crew cut, the route that I'd taken when I followed Dad was called "Dead Man's Path."

"How come you decided to go that way?" he said. "Only a maniac would go that way. You're lucky you didn't die."

"Put a plug in it, Rufus," the chief said.

After that, the officer didn't talk much.

When we finally reached the tower, I noticed ominous clouds on the horizon. I didn't really want to be out here again in the rain. The dark ruin of the tower hung above us.

"So where is it?" the chief said.

I pointed at the sand below the tower. "Somewhere in there."

"Start digging, Rufus," the chief told the officer.

Rufus started digging.

It took another good hour and a half to find what Dad had buried. But it was there—a long sticklike thing wrapped in heavy black plastic.

The chief took photographs, then pulled it out and unrolled the plastic.

We stared for a minute. It was a black-powder rifle. Crudely carved into the stock was a name—EVAN CRANDALL. Dad's name. He must have carved it there thirty years ago. Underneath that were two words, carved with far more care and love:

FIRST SHOT

Something about it made me feel really sad and horrible. There just couldn't be any doubt now, could there? I wondered how he'd felt back when he'd carved it. He must have been expecting a lot out of life when he'd carved those two words. You could almost see the pride, the expectation, the hope, the enthusiasm. My dad wasn't a bad man. I couldn't believe that he was. But something had gone bad wrong.

The chief took some more photos.

"I'll have Rufus take it down to the state, let the crime lab run the ballistics. If it matches up with the bullet that the medical examiner recovered from the autopsy . . ." The chief didn't finish his sentence.

"I'm not sure it's a good idea, you going back to school," he said.

"I live in a dorm," I said. "I barely even see my father."

The chief cleared his throat. "All right," he said finally. "Hopefully we'll get the ballistics report tomorrow. But until then? I don't want you going near your father."

21

It was getting dark as I headed back to The Arsenal. The chief and I had agreed that I would attract less attention if I rode home on my bike rather than getting a ride back with him.

By the time I reached the outskirts of Dartington, the storm clouds that had been coming in from the sea opened up. The temperature must have dropped thirty degrees and the rain started pelting me. I could barely see the road.

After I passed the trailer park where the Jackstaffs lived, I entered a stretch of woods that led out to the school. In the gathering gloom, they seemed full of dark shapes. The road was empty. It was only a few miles to the school—but suddenly I had a feeling of dread in my gut.

I'd just reached the midpoint of the ride when I heard a car approaching me from behind. It had its high beams on. But as it approached all I could see were two bright white cones of light and a dark spot behind the windshield. I expected it to zoom past me. But instead it slowed. I felt the eyes of the driver on me. I looked back again, but the driver's face was invisible, a dark smear behind the rain-streaked windshield.

I felt a jolt of nameless fear and began pedaling harder. The car still didn't pass. I waved it on. But it just matched my speed—no slower, no faster.

The water was coming in torrents now, the wind pushing against me. I felt like I was barely crawling. I stood up on the pedals and started going as fast as I could manage.

The car began creeping closer and closer. Was it just some jerk trying to scare me? Was it the man who'd chased us in the tunnels? Was it my father?

I struggled up the last rise. From here on out, I knew it would be downhill. As I crested the rise, I could barely make out the lights of The Arsenal, glimmering feebly in the dark torrential rain. It still seemed to be about a mile away.

The car pulled up almost even with me. Was the guy toying with me? I could see his outline inside the car, but still couldn't make out any features. He raised his hand. I couldn't tell if he was pointing something at me or what. Was it a gun?

I just couldn't tell.

My heart was hammering like crazy. The dim lights of The Arsenal seemed to be about a million miles away. My lungs were straining and my legs burned.

Inside the car the man was yelling something at me. But

I couldn't make out any sound. *Keep pedaling!* I told myself. *Just keep pedaling!*

I reached the bridge over Kannehutt River, the last major barrier before The Arsenal. The car continued to track me. All he'd have to do was pull over a couple of feet and he'd smash me against the concrete barrier. I'd have no choice but to jump. I could see the river. The sudden downpour had caused it to swell. The black water boiled and raced below me.

I pedaled harder and harder. But it seemed pointless. There was nothing I could do if he wanted to knock me into the water. I could feel my tires skittering and sliding on the wet pavement. If he didn't knock me off, I was liable to lose control myself.

And then I reached the other side.

That was when he made his move. He pulled forward, then edged in front of me, cutting me off.

I had only one hope. I cut the wheel, plunged into the marsh. I felt the front wheel sink into the muck. It was like hitting quicksand. The front wheel simply stopped dead. I flew over the handlebars and went airborne.

22

It took me a minute to get my bearings. I was lying in a pool of water, staring up into the black sky. The raindrops seemed to appear suddenly in midair, then plunged downward, smacking me like falling nails.

I realized that it was the headlights of the car that were making the raindrops seem to materialize above me. I tried to move, but all I could feel was a leaden weariness. It was like my whole life was pressing down on me. My mediocrity, my mom's death—it was all coming down out of the blackness, pinning me to the wet ground.

And then a dark figure emerged from the gloom, stared down at me, and extended his hand. Was this it? I thought. Was this how it would end? Was he going to shoot me, leave me here to rot in the marsh grass, just a few hundred yards from safety?

But the man didn't shoot. In fact, there was nothing in his hand. Instead he said, "You okay, dude?"

"Leo?" I said.

. . .

We put my bike in the trunk of the car Leo was driving—
he said he'd borrowed it from one of his cousins—and we
drove silently toward The Arsenal.

When we reached the gate of the school, I said, "I better
go from here on my own."

I expected him to ask why or to seem insulted that I
didn't want to be seen driving up to the school with him.
But he didn't seem to notice.

"What happened last night?" I said finally.

"Popped him in the face," Leo said. "It knocked his mask
cockeyed and he couldn't see. Then I hauled ass."

"Man," I said. "We thought he'd shot you. I've been feeling like a jerk all day for leaving you down there."

"Really?" he said. "I was feeling exactly the same way.
I felt like I should have done something more to help you.
I was afraid he caught you guys." He sounded distracted
when he said it, though, like it wasn't the main thing on
his mind.

We sat idling in the rain, the windshield wipers going
whackwhackwhackwhack. Finally he spoke.

"Nolan didn't make it," he said.

For a second I wasn't sure what he meant.

"He died," he said. "While we were down there in the
tunnels."

"Oh, man," I said. "I'm so sorry."

"It's just not fair," Leo said.

"Why didn't he get treatment?" I said.

Leo shook his head. "I begged him and begged him. But it seemed like there was something that was eating him. It was like he felt guilty for something and he was trying to make up for it by letting himself die."

"I don't understand."

"I don't know if I do, either. But whatever it was, I think it started when your mom got killed."

Neither of us said anything for a long time.

"You want to know a funny story?" Leo said.

"What's that?"

"A long time ago, there were two brothers. They lived in the village here. One was the good brother and one was the bad brother. They were from a family of fishermen. Lived off the sea. The good brother borrowed some money and bought a big boat. A whaler. Then they went out to catch whales. But they didn't find any whales. And when they came back, a man from Boston came up and demanded the money that he'd lent the good brother for the boat. Well, the brother didn't have it. So the man from Boston said he was going to take the boat.

"That night, the bad brother went out to Jackstaff rock and he put up a lantern and he bobbed it up and down. There was a big storm. In the morning the sun came up and he'd lured a boat in. Everybody in the boat had died, drowned on the rocks. They were all lying there in those rocks. And the sea was dead calm. So the bad brother rowed out and got onto the boat. It turned out that it was a royal mail boat, delivering mail from London to the colonies. And along with the mail was a bag full of gold that was being sent to the king's governor in Boston.

"Well, the bad brother took the money and he gave it to his brother. The good brother paid off the man from Boston and he kept the whaling boat. Meantime, the governor sent up a bunch of soldiers to investigate what had happened to the ship. By that time everybody knew the bad brother had found the money. So the governor's soldiers seized the bad brother, took him back to Boston, and imprisoned him. He got sick and was beaten and so on. And so when he finally got let out of the prison, he came back to Dartington and they say he was a broken man. He couldn't work, and he was bitter and angry.

"Meanwhile, the good brother had made a fortune off the whaling boat. He'd bought two more boats and became this big-cheese rich guy. So the bad brother comes home and asks for some kind of compensation for everything he'd done to help the good brother. But the good brother wouldn't help him out. They got in a big fight. After that night, they never talked again. The good brother moved away. And the bad brother changed his name."

"What was his name?" I said.

"Jackstaff," Leo said. "He changed his last name to Jack-staff."

"No, I mean his original name."

"What do you think?" he said.

I shrugged my shoulders.

"Crandall," Leo said. "His last name was Crandall."

I didn't know what to say. "That was a long time ago," I said.

"There's one thing that seems to have stayed with both families," Leo said. "The Jackstaffs have always been crack shots."

"Is there some point to this story?" I said.

"Nolan, man, he could shoot like crazy. That's what made him such a good poacher."

I sat there listening to the rain beating down on the car.

"I lied to you," Leo said. "I lied to everybody."

"What are you talking about?"

"I never saw your mom."

I turned and looked at him.

"It was Nolan."

I still felt puzzled. What was he getting at?

"Nolan went out that night. He'd been talking about your mom for weeks. You know how if you like a girl, you always find some excuse to bring her up in conversation?"

"Okay . . ."

"For weeks before she died, he kept mentioning your mom. I never knew why. I was just a kid. It seemed weird, you know, him talking about your mom."

"Are you saying they were . . ." I didn't want to say it.

But the truth was, my mom *had* left Dad once. And the time she'd left him, it had been with a guy who was a lot like Nolan.

"What?" Leo said. "Am I saying that your mom was having an affair with him? I don't know. Honestly, I don't think it was like that. I know he was modeling for her. You know, like she was painting a picture of him. But you know how your mom was: she always took people seriously, never acted like she was better than them. A guy like Nolan, been kicked around all his life?—he would have thought she was pretty cool."

I didn't say anything else.

"Anyway," Leo continued, "that night, the night she died, he went out, said he was gonna go hunting. Then he woke me up. I looked at the clock; it was four o'clock in the morning. He had blood on his shirt. At first I thought it was something to do with hunting.

"But then he said, 'Something bad happened.' I was like, 'Dude, I'm sleeping.' But he goes, 'You gotta call the cops.' And then he tells me what I'm supposed to say. How we went out to goof around in the rocks. How I stumbled across your mom." Leo shook his head. The windshield wipers kept going *whackwhackwhackwhack*. "But it was all a lie. I never saw her."

"What happened that night?" I said.

"I don't know," Leo said. "He wouldn't talk about it."

I just sat there, not knowing what to think.

"Whatever's in that safe," Leo said, "it's gotta be the answer. It's gotta explain what happened to your mom."

"Misty and I are gonna go tonight," I said. "You want to come?"

He shook his head. "When I was a kid? When me and you used to play together? My grandma always used to say, 'Jackstaffs and Crandalls don't mix. Nothing good'll ever come of it.'"

I vaguely remembered his grandmother. She used to sit in the trailer where Leo lived when he was a kid, scowling and smoking cigarettes. She had no teeth, so it looked like the whole lower half of her face had been pushed in with a stick. She'd always scared the crap out of me.

"I gotta go," Leo said.

"I'm sorry," I said. "I'm sorry about your brother."

"Yeah," he said. "Well. Stuff happens."

I watched him drive away into the blackness, then I wheeled my bike back to the quad and leaned it against the wall outside my dorm.

As I was getting ready to go into the entrance, I saw Garrett Rothenberg coming out of my house. His dad was with him. The light spilling out of Dad's front room bathed them in this warm yellow glow. The rain had stopped just before they emerged, as though the universe didn't want guys like Garrett and his father getting wet.

I could see Dad silhouetted in the front door, waving after them. There had been a cocktail reception at the house for the board of directors. The Winner and Achiever types had all been invited. I, however, had not. Mr. Rothenberg put his arm around Garrett's shoulders. They were both real good-looking guys, self-confident, smart, rich. I couldn't imagine anything going wrong in their lives. They had it made.

Mr. Rothenberg said something and Garrett laughed loudly, his barking laugh cutting through the air. I caught a glimpse of Dad's face. He was looking at them as they walked away, with this peevish or envious expression on his face. I wondered if that's how my own face looked. I don't know why, but something about it made me want to cry.

23

Misty and I met at about eleven o'clock that night behind Crandall House. She was carrying her rifle.

"What's up with the rifle?" I said.

"Hey, if some jerk-off decides to come after us again tonight, it's gonna be a whole different ball game."

The whole thing gave me a queasy feeling. I told her about running into Leo. She was as relieved as I was to find out that he was still alive. But when I told her that we'd found Dad's old rifle buried in the sand up next to the tower, she seemed kind of sad. "Your dad seems like a good guy," she said. "Kinda stiff, maybe. But . . . do you *really* think he could have killed your mom?"

We were walking through the Barrens out toward Jack-staff Tower. We'd agreed that going back into the tunnels through Dad's office wasn't an option. So the best way in would be through the crack by the tower.

Now that I'd been to the tower with the chief, I was able to find my way out to the point without having to crawl along the cliff. We kept checking behind us to see if anyone was following. But the coast was clear.

Soon we were walking down the tunnel.

It all seemed too easy. We went down the tunnel, we found the little room with the safe in it, we slid the two keys into the safe.

"First this one, then this one," Misty said.

I turned the first key. It turned smoothly. There was a soft click at the end. My palms were sweating. I rubbed them on my pants, inserted the key that Misty had filched from the evidence room, and turned it. Another soft click.

I pulled on the handle and the safe swung slowly open.

"Uh . . ." I said.

"What?"

I looked up at Misty. "It's empty."

It seemed like it took forever to get back to campus that night. We didn't talk. We just trudged along.

When we got back to Crandall House, Misty said, "Well, hey, we tried."

I nodded.

"And, look," she said. "If it was really your dad, that rifle will prove it."

"Yeah, I guess you're right."

Then, "Can I show you something?" I said.

She looked off over my shoulder. "It's late," she said. "I got finals in physics tomorrow."

"Yeah, okay," I said. "Sure. I know."

Then I started to walk away. I felt like a giant weight was smashing down on me, crushing my lungs and my brain and my bones, dragging me into the earth.

"Hold on," she said. "Sure, go ahead and show it to me."

"Wait here," I said.

I snuck up into my room, climbing through the window of the second-floor bathroom—the time-honored method of sneaking in and out of my dorm. Garrett Rothenberg was snoring loudly. I found Mom's digital camera and climbed back down to the quad.

Misty was waiting in the shadows.

We skulked back out to the shooting range, a place we were unlikely to be seen at this hour. Then I took out the camera and turned it on.

"What is it?"

"My mom was an artist," I said. "Dad threw away almost all of her pictures. But Mom took photos of the last few paintings she made. I just thought I'd show them to you."

Misty nodded, but she didn't seem all that interested, I have to admit. It was like she was humoring me because she felt sorry for me.

I pushed the button to scroll through the pictures. The most recent photo showed a small watercolor. It was a picture of a skinny guy with blond hair. Nolan Jackstaff, the way I remembered him. He had his shirt off and the way she'd painted it, you could see his ribs.

I flipped to the next picture. It was another watercolor of Nolan. There were four or five of them in a row. He wasn't wearing his shirt in any of the pictures. Somehow it seemed embarrassing. I suddenly wished I hadn't shown them to Misty.

"Well, anyway . . . " I said. "You got physics in the morning."

"No, hold on." She took the camera and started going through the pictures. She stopped after a couple more and frowned. "Huh," she said.

"What?"

"That looks like you."

I pulled the camera around and stared at the picture. It was a pencil sketch. And it did look like me. Only it wasn't. It was Dad—back when Dad must have been in his twenties. He was smiling broadly, like the happiest man in the world. I had almost forgotten that guy.

"He used to smile like that," I said. "Back before she . . . died." I kept looking at the picture. "The odd thing, though," I said, "is that she must have done this back when they first met."

"Why's that odd?"

"Well, usually she just photographed all her most recent pictures. Then she'd download them to the computer. That way she had a record of everything she'd done. But once they were on the computer, why take another picture?"

Misty didn't say anything. She just pushed the button to move on to the next picture. "Where's that?" she said. "Doesn't look like anything around here."

And it wasn't. It was a sketch of a little hotel that we'd stayed in when we went on a vacation to France. Back when I was five. "Another old picture," I said.

"Maybe it was like her greatest hits," she said.

We kept flipping through the pictures. Occasionally Misty would say, "Nice," or "Isn't that pretty?"

Then we got to the end. There was an image of a wall, a chair, a lamp. I was about to skip past it. But then I realized what it was.

"That's not a picture," I said. "That's a video." Mom's camera could shoot cheap, grainy-looking videos as well as still photos.

I hit the button that made it play.

I felt a strange tug. Mom's voice! She wasn't in the frame, but I could hear her talking. I didn't think I'd ever hear it again. Her voice sounded tinny coming out of the dinky little speaker. But it brought back a wash of feelings—not specific memories, just that feeling of security that I'd felt before all this bad stuff happened.

"Hold on, hold on," Mom said. Who was she talking to? But then I remembered: there was a particular way of talking, a tone of voice she used when she was painting and talking to herself. The camera shook, then steadied. Mom appeared in the middle of the frame. She wore a white dress with little blue spots on it. This must have been taken the day she was killed!

"It's all in the pictures," she said. Then she held up a painting—a watercolor picture of a skinny blond guy. Nolan. "I had been storing them in a safe. But now I'm not so sure that's the best place." She was carrying a picture in her hand. "Now you see it," she said, holding up the picture. Then she turned the painting around. "Now you don't."

Then she walked closer to the camera and reached out toward the lens. She must have set it up on a tripod, started it recording—and now she was reaching out to turn it off.

And there, my mom's face froze forever, slightly out of focus, holding the back of this picture out toward the camera. The last image she left on the planet.

"What's she mean?" Misty said. "'It's all in the pictures'?"

"I don't know."

We flipped through the pictures. But there seemed to be no rhyme or reason to them. They were just old pictures.

"Maybe it's some kind of code," Misty said.

I shook my head. "Nah. My mom didn't have the patience to do a crossword puzzle. And she hated math. Codes just weren't her thing."

"Then what?"

"No clue."

Misty squinted at the picture. "Maybe it's something on

the actual pictures." She stared closely at the picture Mom was holding.

"Any way to zoom in?"

"I don't think so. Why?"

"Look on the back." She pointed at the blurry little image. "It looks like something's glued onto the back of the painting."

I stared at the picture. It was hard to tell. The quality of the videos taken by the little point-and-shoot camera was pretty pathetic. But, yeah, it did look like there was a piece of paper stuck to the back of the painting. A piece of paper covered with writing. It wasn't possible to make anything else out of it.

"That paper wasn't there on the painting found on her body," I said. "I saw it and it wasn't there."

"Maybe somebody peeled it off."

I kept frowning at the picture. "I don't know," I said. "I don't really see what would be relevant about it."

"Maybe it's some kind of clue," Misty said. "A page from a book or something. A diary. A notebook. Who knows? Whatever it was, she'd been storing it in the safe. Then she thought somebody was coming after her, and that maybe they'd find them there. So she decided to hide them in plain sight. She glued them onto the backs of all these pictures. Each painting that she took a photo of with this camera has one of . . . well . . . whatever's on that piece of paper."

My eyes widened. It sounded plausible.

"So Nolan gave you the key," Misty continued, "because he thought these papers or book pages or whatever were still in the safe. He didn't realize your mom had moved them right before she was killed." Misty grinned broadly. "So all we have to do is find the pictures!"

I felt a wave of despair run through me. I shook my head.

"What?" she said.

"Dad threw them all away."

"No!"

She blinked. And I think we probably had the exact same thought at the exact same moment. "He found them," we both said.

Misty nodded glumly. "Whatever the clues were, your dad found them. Then he ditched the paintings."

We sat silently for a minute.

"This sucks," I said.

"Yeah. Yeah, it does." She stood. "Well, we better go get some sleep. I don't want to fall asleep in physics."

"Yeah," I said. "Plus, we've got the shoot-out tomorrow to see who's gonna be First Shot."

She gave me a haughty look. "Is there any doubt?" she said. "I'm gonna cream you."

Then she walked away.

Yeah, I thought, *she probably is going to cream me.*

24

The next morning, I took my final exam in ancient history. Oddly enough, I aced it. The main question was about Julius Caesar. I'd read the book Dad had given me, Caesar's *Conquest of Gaul,* about three times. It was a totally cool book. Caesar had dictated the book himself, and so when you got done with it, you felt almost like you actually knew the guy.

I came out of the test feeling really psyched. For about ten minutes there, I'd actually forgotten about Mom, about the rifle, about the tunnels and the safe and the pictures that Dad had destroyed.

And then I saw Chief Dowd. He was leaning against his car. His entire police force—all three officers—were with him. He motioned to me.

I walked over to him and he sighed. "Well," he said, "the crime lab worked all night. They ran the ballistics . . ."

I didn't want to hear the rest.

"The rifle matches," he said. "It was your dad."

I put my head in my hands.

"I've been in contact with the state social services department. They're gonna send a caseworker over to talk to you
so you can figure out what's going to happen to you after
this. Hopefully you can stay here at the school for a little
while. After that?" He cleared his throat.

I hadn't even thought about that. If Dad went to jail,
where would I live? I didn't have any living relatives at all.
No cousins, no uncles or aunts, no living grandparents. Who
would take care of me? I would be turning eighteen within
a year. I was pretty sure that would mean I'd be on my own.
Would I have to get a job? Find my own place to live? Buy
all my own food and clothes? Would I even be able to go to
college? The whole thing gave me a panicky feeling.

"We're going to go arrest him now," the chief said. He
looked at me for a long time, chewing sadly on the corner
of his gray mustache. "Anything I can do for you?"

My mind was a total blank. *Do* for me? What could you
possibly do for a kid in my shoes? What could you possibly
do that would make a difference in my life?

"Can I talk to him?" I said.

"I don't think that's a great idea."

"He killed my mom!" I said. "Can't I at least ask him
why?"

A calculating look came into the chief's eye. "You know
what . . ." he said.

25

It didn't occur to me until later why the chief let me talk to Dad. The truth was, they didn't have a rock-solid case here. They had a rifle. And they had my word that Dad had put it there. But they didn't have a motive or a videotape of the crime. They didn't have a witness.

A confession would have been handy. And I think the chief thought maybe I could help him get one.

They led Dad out of Crandall House. You could tell he was handcuffed—though they'd let him put a coat over his hands to cover the cuffs. To save him the embarrassment. Yeah, right.

It seemed like the entire student body was suddenly in the quad. I guess the word must have spread somehow. It was completely silent. Everyone stared as two officers led my father down the worn marble steps of Crandall House. I could feel my blood rushing in my veins, hear a roaring in my ears. Dad was wearing his usual tweed jacket and bow tie, his collar crisp, his shoes shined. He was looking off fixedly at the horizon. His head was high, but his cheeks were pale. He seemed a little wobbly when he walked, like he was about to faint. I've never seen anybody going to a firing squad—but I'd imagine that's how they would look. They took him to one of the patrol cars and opened the back door.

He paused. For a moment his eyes met mine. I don't know what I expected, but there seemed to be nothing in them—he didn't look accusatory, didn't look sad, didn't look regretful. Just a blank emptiness. They could have been the eyes of a doll.

As he folded into the car and the door thunked shut behind him, I noticed Garrett Rothenberg standing about thirty feet away from me. Misty was standing next to him. Garrett said something to her, then a smirk appeared on the corner of his mouth.

She turned and slapped him. "You're a *moe*-ron," she said loudly. Then she turned and looked around at all the gawking kids and shouted. "All of you! You're all *moe*-rons! What are you staring at?"

It was then that I realized they weren't staring at Dad anymore.

They were staring at *me*.

• • •

So I guess you could say I was feeling pretty sorry for myself by the time I was sitting in the little interview room in the police station. Sorry for myself and mad, too.

How could he have done this to me?

I was all worked up by the time they led him in. He was cuffed and there was black stuff on his hands from the fingerprinting process.

He sat down and looked at me without speaking. The chief stood behind Dad.

"Why?" I said finally.

He just kept looking at me. Finally he said, "David, I don't know what you want from me."

"I just want to know why! Was she having an affair with Nolan Jackstaff? Did she find out something about you that made you look bad? What? What could have possibly been so bad that you had to shoot her in the heart?"

He licked his lips and frowned. He seemed to be thinking hard about something. Finally he said, "David, you don't have to go through this."

"Go through *what*?" I shouted.

Dad waggled one hand at me. It seemed to be encompassing everything in the room. "This . . . *this* . . ."

"This *what*?"

"This . . . performance."

I stared at him. "Is that what you think this is? A performance? You really are a sick dude, that's all I have to say."

"David . . ." He seemed to be pleading to me with his eyes. "David, please . . ."

"Don't turn this on *me*!" I said. "I lost my mother. Can you even imagine that?"

He shook his head, sighed. "No, I guess not."

"Then just tell me. Tell me why!"

Dad turned to the chief. "Look, whatever you want. I'll say whatever you want. Just . . . please don't make me do this in front of my son."

The chief suddenly had a triumphant gleam in his eye. "Are you saying you murdered your wife?"

"Don't make me do this in front of my son," Dad repeated.

The chief nodded. "Okay. David, you need to go now."

But I wasn't finished. "Fine!" I said. "You did what you did. But did you have to wipe her memory off the map, too?"

Dad looked puzzled.

I was furious. "Oh, don't give me that!" I shouted. "All I had left of her were those paintings. Why'd you destroy them?"

Dad looked even more puzzled. "Destroy?" he said.

"Are you gonna lie about that, too?"

He cocked his head slightly. "I never said I *destroyed* them, David. I said I *disposed* of them."

I stared at him.

"They're in that mini-storage warehouse over on the road

to Lewiston. I just couldn't stand looking at them anymore. They're all there. All of them."

"David," the chief said, "you need to go."

Half an hour later, the chief came out with a piece of paper in his hands. He didn't seem to want to meet my eye.

"He confessed?" I said.

The chief nodded, held up the paper in his hands. "It's all right here."

"Why?" I said. "Why did he do it?"

The chief stopped, turned toward me, then shook his head. "He wouldn't say."

"Can I ask you another question?"

"Sure, son."

"Why did you come out to our house and ask to do a search back in August? Why then? It had been over two years since Mom died."

The chief smiled ruefully. "Your mother is the only murder we've had here in this town since I've been chief of police. Which is quite a few years. So it's been bothering me like heck that I couldn't solve it. So one day back in August I just pulled out every single scrap of paper and every piece of evidence that I had relating to the case, then I closed the door to my office and started going over it piece by piece. And I just couldn't see anybody who was a legitimate suspect besides your father. So I decided I'd go out there and rattle his cage."

"But you said you had a witness. . . ."

The chief's shoulders went up and down a fraction of an inch. "Hey, I just wanted to see how he responded. If I'd had a witness . . . I'd have been out there with a search warrant. But the truth is, I had nothing. Until you came to me."

I left the police department feeling nauseated, and my left hand was trembling slightly. So I had done it. I'd put my own father in prison. I should have felt good about it. I mean, he deserved it, right? But instead I just felt like I'd done something terrible.

26

I went back to school with this weird hollow feeling in my chest. I'd finished all the exams. There was nothing left to do before graduation.

Nothing left except the contest to see who'd be First Shot.

I wasn't sure I could do it. Wasn't sure I could even touch my rifle.

It was the oddest thing. I came back to campus and nobody said a word to me. I mean, everybody knew what had happened. But no one said a word to me. Not, "Sorry to hear about what happened to your dad." Not, "You gonna be okay?" Not, "Have you got somewhere to stay?" Nothing. They all just looked away.

I went back to my dorm room and even Rothenberg didn't speak. Which was some kind of record, because Rothenberg had something to say about everything. He just sat there, looked up from his desk, then started tapping his pencil on the desk.

"I'm gonna go to the library, study over there."

"What?" I said. "Am I creeping you out or something? I'm not gonna bite you."

He didn't answer, just scooped up his calculus book and headed into the hallway.

I sat on the bed and stared at the wall. I don't know what I thought about. Nothing really. My mind was just a blank. I felt this strange calm. Calmness and blankness and emptiness.

After a minute I picked up my mom's camera and started looking at the pictures. Soon the LOW BATTERY symbol flicked on in the corner of the screen. But I kept looking. Eventually the battery got so low that the screen kept flickering off.

I remembered there was a second battery in Rothenberg's drawer. I pulled it open and saw the big stack of letters from his dad. I felt this strange, resentful feeling again, remembering the way he and his dad had come out of the reception at my father's house the other night, the light around them, Mr. Rothenberg's arm around Garrett's neck, the private joke they were having. . . .

Normally I wouldn't do a thing like this. But for some reason I just felt this huge burst of jealousy, and I pulled out one of the letters from his dad and opened it up.

The letter was printed on the stationery of his dad's company. At the top the words ROTHENBERG, LYTTLE & COMPANY, FUND MANAGERS were embossed into the paper, which was so thick and creamy that it almost seemed like a piece of hand-tooled leather. I wasn't sure what a fund manager was . . . but I knew it had to do with money. Lots of money. For about half a second, I felt bad reading his personal letters. But not *that* bad. Like I mentioned before, Garrett used to read my e-mails and stuff all the time.

What I read came as kind of a shock.

The whole letter was devoted to belittling Garrett, telling him how he wasn't smart enough, didn't work hard enough, all kinds of stuff like that. I mean, my dad's a pain in the neck sometimes. But this was crazy. Hey, Garrett was number three in the class, captain of the soccer team, all that kind of crap. I mean, *my* dad actually had good reason to rag on me sometimes. Whereas his dad just seemed to be doing it for sport.

I opened another letter. Same deal. One nasty thing after another, Mr. Rothenberg haranguing Garrett about his character, his intelligence, his friends—basically there was no aspect of his character that his dad couldn't find fault with.

Kind of gave me a new perspective on the guy. I almost felt sorry for him.

Almost.

But right then I was too busy feeling sorry for myself.

I put the letters away, found the other camera battery, and loaded it into the camera. As I was about to turn it back on, I heard a soft knock on the door. I looked up and there was Misty, standing in the doorway.

"You okay?" she said.

"You're not supposed to be here," I said. The Arsenal had a strict policy, no girls in the boys' dorm and vice versa.

"What are they gonna do?" she said. "Throw me out of school?"

She sat down on Garrett Rothenberg's bed and looked at me. "I'm sorry," she said. "I don't even know what to say."

"Yeah." I kept looking at my mom's paintings.

"Could you turn that thing off?" she said.

I turned it off, lay back in my own bed, and stared up at the ceiling. Then I told Misty everything that had happened—that my dad had confessed, that the ballistics matched the rifle buried by the tower, everything. I paused. "I guess the only nice thing, turns out he didn't burn Mom's pictures. They're in a mini-storage warehouse."

Misty was looking at me with an odd frown on her face. "Don't you want to know *why*?" she said finally.

I shrugged. "Why what?"

"Why he killed her."

I shrugged. "Sure."

"Then let's go," she said.

"Go where?"

She poked me in the arm with one long red fingernail. "To the mini-storage place, you *moe*-ron! Let's look at the paintings."

I don't know why, but for some reason I'd almost forgotten about the paintings—about the clues that Mom and Nolan may (or may not) have attached to them.

I sighed. "What's the point?"

Misty slapped me on the leg. "Come on. Get up. Let's go."

"I don't even know where the key is."

"I said, let's go."

Twenty minutes later I was pulling Dad's Volvo into the mini-storage warehouse on the highway outside Darting-ton. I'd found his spare keys on the ring hanging inside his office door at home. There was a black iron fence around the outside, but the gate was open. Several rows of cheap concrete buildings were laid out on a concrete slab, just enough room between them so that you could drive your car through. It was like rows of tiny little garages, each with a door that you could pull up into the ceiling.

"Look for number forty-two," I said.

All my dad's spare keys had been neatly labeled, including one that said MINI-STORAGE #42.

Misty pointed. "There."

I pulled the Volvo in front of the garage door with 42 painted on it in large orange letters. We hopped out and checked the door. It was locked at the bottom with a small padlock. I slid the key into the lock. It was a little rusty, like the lock hadn't been used in a long time. But it opened fine. I took off the lock, then Misty leaned over and pulled up the door, revealing a room exactly the width of the door and about ten feet deep.

All the paintings my mom had ever done were stacked up in the back on a set of cheap metal shelves.

A painting of Nolan Jackstaff was lying on one of the lower shelves. Misty saw it at the same time I did. She picked it up, turned it around. On the back there was a piece of typing paper, neatly taped to the larger, heavier watercolor paper.

Misty carefully peeled it off with her long red fingernails.

"Can I ask you a question?" I said.

Misty looked up at me.

"How do you expect people to take you seriously?" I said. "All that makeup? The red fingernails? If I didn't know you, I'd think you were a total bimbo."

"You been wanting to ask me that all term, haven't you?" she said.

I nodded.

"That's just how it's done in Mississippi," she said. "A girl wouldn't consider going out without her face on."

"Yeah, but—"

"It's amazing the stuff you can get away with when people underestimate you," she said. "You should know."

"What do you mean?"

"There's a lot more to *you* than meets the eye." I wasn't

sure if that was a compliment or not. Before I could ask for a clarification, she held up the piece of paper. "This mean anything to you?"

I looked at it. Rows and rows of numbers.

"Some kind of spreadsheet," I said.

"No duh!" she said.

"Oh. You mean like what are the numbers *about*?"

"Sh'yeah!" she said sarcastically.

I shrugged.

As it turned out, all the pictures from the camera were clumped together. It took us about fifteen minutes to get all the pieces of paper organized. There were about forty or fifty of them. Most were like the first we'd found. Some kind of accounting stuff. It was all really old, though, dated about fifteen years ago.

"I think it's some kind of accounting stuff related to The Arsenal," Misty said. "Something to do with investments."

I was still turning pictures over, looking to see if there was anything else. I found one last piece of paper. As it happened, it was taped to the sketch of my dad, the one where he was smiling, looking all happy and carefree.

"Well, that's weird," I said. It was a letter. A letter on fancy stationery so heavy and soft and creamy that it felt like tooled leather.

"A letter," I said. "It's a letter from Rothenberg's dad."

"What's it say?"

I started reading. It was addressed to my grandfather.

"Dear Grant: I'm troubled to hear the bizarre allegations you've made regarding my firm's management of the school's investment funds—"

I broke off.

A shadow had fallen across the concrete floor of the little room. Misty turned around. A man stood there, looking into the room. He smiled broadly.

"Well, well," he said. "Speak of the devil, huh?"

"Mr. *Rothenberg*?" I said.

Two men stepped out from behind Mr. Rothenberg. They were both large men—one of them merely very big, while the second guy was downright *huge*—both wearing suits, both wearing sunglasses, both wearing little things in their ears with curlicue wires running down their necks into the collars. And they both carried pistols.

"You know what I hate?" Mr. Rothenberg said. "I hate Volvos."

I stared at him.

"Nick," Mr. Rothenberg said, turning to one of the men behind him, "get rid of the Volvo. Drive it off a cliff or something."

"Wait a minute, wait a minute," I said. I was trying to make sense of the whole thing. What were they doing here?

Mr. Rothenberg stepped briskly into the room, hand extended toward the pile of papers that Misty and I had just peeled off the backs of all those paintings. "You don't know *how* long I've been looking for that stuff. I've had *professionals* on it!" He was still smiling. It was the same big phony smile that Garrett always seemed to wear on his face. "And here a couple of *kids* turn the stuff up! It's a remarkable world, isn't it?"

He tried to grab the pieces of paper, but Misty got to them first. She shoved them down the front of her blouse, glaring angrily at Mr. Rothenberg.

"It was *you*," she said. "Wasn't it?"

"Me what?" he said.

"You killed David's mom."

"Oh, come on, don't be a chump. Guys like me don't have to do things like that. That's why they invented money. So you could *buy* people instead of shooting them." He seemed to think everything he said was totally hilarious. He laughed loudly.

Outside, the guy Mr. Rothenberg had referred to as Nick got into Dad's car. There was something about the way he moved. It was then that I realized . . . *he was the guy from the tunnel! The guy who had been chasing us*. The door slammed, then the Volvo drove quickly away.

"Wait!" I yelled.

But the car was gone.

"You know why I hate Volvos?" Mr. Rothenberg held up his hand. "Hey, actually I don't care if you want to know or not, because I'm gonna tell you anyway. The reason I hate Volvos is because they're the *safety* car." He pronounced the word *safety* with a sarcastic twist. "People are like, 'Hey, drive a Volvo, you'll never die. You'll never lose your precious child in an accident, you'll never get colon cancer, you'll never fall off a trampoline and break your neck.'"

"Why'd you do it?" I said. I was finally seeing it now. It wasn't my dad at all. It was him. "My mom was a nice person."

"Your mom was a nosy little twit." Mr. Rothenberg laughed. "But shut up, kid. I'm telling a story. The reason I hate Volvos is because they perpetuate the stupid, stupid, childish idea that life can be somehow free of risk. Come on, people! Life is nothing *but* risk. Bad things happen all the time. Volvos roll over and catch fire and beautiful little children get roasted to death like marshmallows. Hey, kids, that's life!"

Then he stepped toward Misty, hand extended toward the papers that were now hidden beneath her blouse. She took a step back.

"Jerry," Mr. Rothenberg said. "Isn't it quaint, what this girl just did? Sticking the papers down her blouse? Like our sense of decency might stop us from reaching down the shirt of a sweet little teenager?"

The huge guy named Jerry laughed obligingly. But you could tell he just laughed because he was paid to.

"Take the papers, Jerry," Mr. Rothenberg said. "Then put 'em in the car."

Misty was backed up against the shelves now. I wanted

to do something to help her. But I couldn't seem to make myself move. I felt frozen. It wasn't exactly fear. It was just like every nerve in my brain had been body-slammed so bad that I couldn't even think.

"Get away from me, you big *moe*-ron," Misty said. She didn't look scared. She just looked pissed.

The big guy stepped quickly toward her. He must have been like six-foot-seven and well over three hundred pounds.

"Don't make me mess you up, sweetie," the guy said. He didn't seem malicious the way he said it. Just like it was business.

Misty swallowed. Then she reached inside her blouse, held out the papers.

The big guy nodded and extended his hand.

Which gave Misty the opening she was waiting for. She kicked that big guy in the nuts so hard, he must have gotten bumps on the inside of his head. He groaned and clutched at his crotch. Problem was, he still had the gun.

I don't know why, but suddenly I had an idea. "Push him!" I shouted. Then I jumped down behind the big guy, got on my hands and knees. The old playground trick.

Misty didn't need any prompting. She put both palms on his chest and heaved. The big guy fell over backward, tripping over my body and falling with a huge *SLAMMM!* into the floor. His head did that coconut thing, bouncing off the floor. After that he didn't even move. The pistol skittered across the concrete. Misty jumped over the huge man and headed for the door. And I was right behind her. I scooped up the huge man's gun.

Mr. Rothenberg stepped backward, eyes wide. He didn't look scared, just kind of surprised. I pointed the gun at him.

There was a big Lincoln Navigator idling about ten feet away. "Let's go!" Misty shouted, jumping into the driver's seat.

I jumped into the passenger seat and she stomped on the gas.

Outside, Mr. Rothenberg looked at us. He had that big smile on his face again. "Okay," he said pleasantly, "now I'm starting to get mildly peeved."

He was flipping out his cell phone as we skidded away.

"So," I said as we thundered, "I guess your dad taught you all kinds of racecar-driving tricks?"

She slammed into a bunch of garbage cans.

"Not so much," she said, pulling out onto the highway. "Matter of fact, I've never driven a car in my life." She grinned fiercely. "I played *Grand Theft Auto* a few times, though."

"Maybe you better pull over and let me drive, then," I said. I could see the speedometer. She was already going sixty-five miles an hour. "Supposedly these big SUVs roll over pretty easy."

"Okay," she said, cutting the wheel.

Apparently the cars in *Grand Theft Auto* work a little differently than real-life Lincoln Navigators. Because the next thing I knew the car was making this terrible screeching noise, and then we were rolling over and over and over, and we were surrounded in a cocoon of terrible noises—glass shattering, metal crunching, rubber squealing.

Then suddenly I was upside down and the air bag in front of me was deflating. And it was completely silent.

"You okay?" I said.

Misty lay in a heap on the ceiling. Which was now the floor. I had put my seat belt on but she hadn't. So when the Navigator started rolling, she had flown around the cabin. There were cuts on her face, blood dripping onto her blouse. For a long time she didn't move.

Finally she looked over and said, "Maybe I ought to take a few lessons before I try that again."

28

The next hour was kind of surreal. We ended up in the hospital. Neither of us was hurt all that badly. But Mr. Rothenberg had arrived at the wreck at the same time as Chief Dowd and the ambulance. Mr. Rothenberg started ordering everybody around, telling them how they had to take care of "these precious young people" and all this other crap. I guess Misty and I were both a little out of it, because we basically let them strap us to gurneys and haul us off to the hospital.

I kept trying to tell Chief Dowd all this stuff about how Mr. Rothenberg had killed my mom and everything. But the chief acted like I was delirious and pretty much ignored me.

We had lost the gun in the wreck. But the one good thing was that Misty still had the papers. She kept holding onto them the whole time, wouldn't let the ambulance guys take them away. Next thing I knew, we were lying in the ER in a couple of beds right next to each other.

And Mr. Rothenberg was rushing around telling everybody how he was going to pay for our care, how he wanted the best medical treatment humanly possible, how he was going to sue the hospital if there was even a hair on our heads that got hurt, on and on and on. It was like the guy never shut up. Come to think of it, he was exactly like Garrett.

And as soon as the nurses and doctors went away, he walked over to us and said, "How'm I doing, kids? You'd think I actually cared, huh?"

"Kiss my grits," Misty said.

Mr. Rothenberg winked at me. "Love those little Southern girls, huh?" Then he yanked the curtain around us so that nobody could see what he was doing and pulled out a gun. I think it was the same one we'd had earlier. It must have flown out the window of the Navigator while we were crashing. He pointed it at Misty. "Okey-dokey, sweetheart. Let's have the papers."

I could see Misty considering her options.

But before anything even happened, we heard footsteps coming rapidly toward us. Mr. Rothenberg hastily hid the pistol. Someone pulled the curtain back. It was one of the doctors, a short black guy who sounded like he was from Jamaica.

Misty sat up in the bed, let her feet dangle off the side. "We're gonna go now, Doctor," she said.

The doctor shook his head. "I would highly recommend against that," he said.

"It's all right, Doctor," Mr. Rothenberg said brightly. "You've done a fabulous job treating these young folks. But I think we can all see they're just fine. I'll see them to the door."

"I'm afraid there will be a great deal of paperwork before they can—"

Mr. Rothenberg cut him off. "Paperwork's my specialty, Doctor. Besides, these young people have an important appointment at two o'clock."

My eyebrows must have risen slightly.

"What!" Mr. Rothenberg said to me. "You think I'd let you two kids be late for the contest? Everybody wants to find out who's gonna be First Shot. I wouldn't let you miss that, not in a million years." He put one finger in the middle of the doctor's chest, poked him gently. "Now, Doctor, if you'd kindly step aside . . ."

Misty stood unsteadily, stumbled against the doctor, then headed toward the door.

"I need to talk to my dad," I said to Misty as we walked out the front door of the hospital.

She looked at her watch. "The competition is in, like, an hour."

"This is kinda more important, you know?" I said.

She nodded and smiled sadly. "Yeah, I guess so. I'll have your rifle ready. As soon as you're done, come straight to the firing range." Then she handed me the papers we'd peeled off the back of Mom's pictures.

There was a cab waiting outside the hospital, a purple-and-green minivan that looked like somebody had beat it up with a baseball bat. She hopped in and the taxi drove off, the engine farting and belching smoke. Dartington is a small town, so the police station is only a few hundred yards from the hospital.

I walked in and the little cow bell clanked over the door. As soon as the clerk at the front desk saw me, she called, "Chief!"

Chief Dowd came out and said, "Hello, son."

"I want to talk to my dad," I said.

He shook his head. "I'm sorry, he's about to be transported to the Devonshire county jail."

"Just five minutes," I said.

"Look, we're on a schedule here—"

"For God's sake!" I said. "I'm about to lose my dad for the rest of my life. You think you could have just a tiny bit of compassion?" Usually I wouldn't talk to a grown-up like that. But having your dad charged with murder?—it kind of changes your perspective a little.

The chief sighed. "All right. Five minutes."

He frisked me, took away the pen and the key ring in my pocket, then led me back to the little cell where Dad was sitting. It was an old cell with steel bars. Dad was on a cot bolted to the wall. He sat with his hands folded and his eyes closed. He could have been praying or sleeping—it was hard to know.

"Sit here," the chief said, putting a folding chair in front of the cell. "You can talk through the bars."

I sat down and waited until the chief went away.

"What the hell are you doing, Dad?" I said finally.

That got his eyes to open nice and quick! "Excuse me?" he said sharply.

"You didn't kill Mom," I said.

He just looked at me.

"Why did you confess?" I said.

He had a strange, tortured expression on his face as he stared at me. "You have to ask?" he said.

I stared back. "Something wrong with your hearing?" I was feeling really pissed. At him. At Mr. Rothenberg. At Chief Dowd. At pretty much the whole world. It all seemed mixed up and crazy.

"You know why," he said softly. His eyes were so sad-looking, I couldn't believe it. Sad, and a little disappointed.

"Wait a minute!" I said. "Wait a minute."

He kept looking at me with this sad expression. Maybe I'm a doofus, but it only hit me just then.

"Dad? You think *I* did it?"

He gave me this kind of weird, ghostly, sad smile. But he didn't say anything.

"You told the cops that you did it because . . ." And then it hit me, bam, right between the eyes. "You confessed so that *I* wouldn't get charged with killing her? That's crazy! Dad, I didn't kill her! Why would you ever think such a thing?"

He didn't say a word, just kept looking at me with this ghostly smile.

"Say it!" I shouted. "You think I did it? You better tell me why!"

He took a deep breath. "It's okay," he said. "After I lost your mother, I've just felt like I was sleepwalking. I don't care about much of anything anymore. Whatever happened between you and your mom—I'm sure it was an accident. I know you wouldn't have harmed her on purpose."

I stared at him.

"It's okay, son. I know you had the big fight with her that day." He shrugged. "Still, I didn't even consider the possibility. Not until I noticed that my rifle was out of place. As you know, I never use it. Haven't fired it in twenty-five years. The next day I saw that it was out of place. So I smelled the barrel. There was a fresh smell of gunpowder. It had obviously just been fired."

I shook my head, trying to figure everything out.

Dad kept going. "I didn't shoot the gun, son. So who else could it have been? No one else had the key to our house. By process of deduction, it had to be you."

He looked at the floor for a minute. Finally he said, "I thought it was all over. Until the chief came out that night and started talking about a search warrant. I knew then that if he came back and found it . . . well, obviously someone had tipped him off. There must have been a witness. Somebody who had seen you do it, but never spoken up. I figured Chief Dowd would be back with a warrant. So I took it out to the Barrens and buried it."

I just sat there shaking my head.

"You're going to be fine, son," Dad said. "I still love you. No matter what you did, what kind of mistakes you made . . . I'll love you forever."

I leaned toward him and I said, "How could you think I'd do a thing like that?"

He met my eye.

"Dad, I didn't shoot her. Okay?"

"You don't have to—"

"Dad! Listen to me! I didn't kill Mom. She found something. Her and Nolan Jackstaff."

At the mention of Nolan Jackstaff, Dad's face hardened slightly.

"Nolan Jackstaff used to mess around down in the tunnels. There's an old safe down there. He found it. I think he found the keys for it, too, and he found something in the safe. Something about the money that Grandpa Boyce supposedly stole from the school."

At the mention of Mom's father he sat up suddenly. "How did you know about—"

"Mr. Entwhistle told me."

Dad frowned. "But—"

"Dad, I think you got framed. I think Nolan took the stuff he found to Mom. He probably could see there was something weird about it. But he probably didn't know what. He was modeling for her. And he figured since Mom worked in the accounting department for the school, she would be able to tell him what the stuff meant. Which she did."

"I don't understand. Why would anybody care? Grandpa Boyce . . . well, we didn't want to tell you about any of that—but Grandpa Boyce killed himself after he admitted to the board of directors that he'd taken all that money."

"What if he didn't, though?"

"Didn't what?"

"What if he *didn't* take the money? What if somebody else did?"

"That doesn't make sense. Why would he say he did it if . . . "

"He was framed. He was blackmailed. Whatever you want to call it. He was trying to protect the reputation of the school."

"But then . . . if he didn't take the money, who did?"

Before I could say, Chief Dowd came into the room. "Okay, Mr. Crandall," he said, "it's time."

"Who?" Dad repeated.

"Mr. Crandall, you need to turn around and put your hands through the slot so I can place the handcuffs on you."

"I'm gonna figure it all out," I said. "Don't worry, Dad, I'm gonna get you out."

Dad turned around and slid his hands out the little slot in the bars, let Chief Dowd put the cuffs on him. When he turned back, there were tears running down his face. "You didn't do it, son?" he said.

"Of course not! God!"

It was the weirdest thing. Here he was about to get sent off to jail, charged with killing his own wife, hands shackled, wearing an orange prison jumpsuit and a tacky-looking pair of flip-flops—and he looked like the most relieved guy on the planet. Strange. I hadn't seen him cry since Mom died, not once. For three years he'd been like a block of wood. And now, suddenly, this. It was bizarre.

Chief Dowd clamped one hand on my shoulder. "You need to go now, son."

I caught the same rattletrap purple-and-green cab back to campus that Misty had taken. It was driven by an Indian guy with a really large gold watch.

"Big excitement at the school, hey?" he said cheerily.

"I guess," I said.

"My goodness, the headmaster of such a prestigious institution! Charged with murder!"

I didn't say anything, but the cabdriver apparently liked to talk a lot.

"I drove the headmaster to the school once. He was quite pleasant to me. Gave me a ten-dollar tip. Which is quite generous, I must tell you. Did you come into contact with him often?"

"You could say that," I said.

"And what about you, young sir?" the cabdriver said. "Your appraisal of the man? Would you have suspected him to be capable of such a heinous act?"

Yeah. Yeah, I guess I would have. And I'd have been wrong. What was wrong with me? What was wrong with him? How could either of us have suspected the other of doing a thing like that?

"He didn't do it," I said.

"You know this for a fact?" The driver grinned at me in the mirror.

"Just drive," I said. "I'm already running late."

29

I sprinted all the way to the rifle range, arrived three minutes late. The contest was a big deal, so all of the faculty and
most of the student body were lined up on the side of the
range or sitting on the grassy bank beside the range, watching. Three judges, wearing blue blazers with the crest of
The Arsenal on the breast pocket, stood behind the shooting line. Colonel Taylor stood beside them wearing his dress
uniform, a clipboard in his hand, a cigar in his mouth.

Colonel Taylor gave me his angry General Patton face as
I raced to the line.

"You're late, for cripe's sake, Crandall!" he said. "That's
an automatic disqualification."

"I had to talk to my dad," I said. "At the jail."

It was a perfect day, no clouds in the sky, the temperature warm but not excessive, no wind. The crowd watched
us silently. I could feel their eyes on me, pitying me, despis-
ing me—I didn't really know. All I knew was that I felt a

vague sense of shame and humiliation, like I was standing there naked in front of all those people.

Colonel Taylor took his cigar out of his mouth, glared at me. "Well. I suppose under the circumstances . . . " He scowled, looked me up and down. "Where's your rifle?"

Misty held it up. "Right here, sir."

"All right, then." He put the cigar back in his mouth and marched down the line with his clipboard. "Here are your shooting-lane assignments!" he barked. "Lane one, Cleary. Lane two, Crandall. Lane three, Judge. Lane four . . . "

I walked over and got my rifle from Misty. "Thanks," I said.

"How's your dad doing?" she said.

I shrugged. "Let's just shoot," I said. "We'll talk about it later."

". . . lane ten," Colonel Taylor said, "Rothenberg."

Everybody got in their shooting lanes. The targets had already been set up, fifty yards out. Simple circular targets just a little bigger than a grapefruit. A bunch of circles with a black dot in the middle—the ten ring. Now that I'd been shooting with Misty at one hundred yards, the target seemed laughably close and easy.

"Ladies and gentlemen," Colonel Taylor continued, "you are about to compete for the most treasured honor in the history of The Arsenal. For two hundred and seven years, ten students have competed each year, with the winner firing First Shot at commencement.

"The rules of the contest are simple," Colonel Taylor barked. "You will be permitted ten shots. I will call the shots. Each time I call the shot, you will have ten seconds to shoot. If you fail to shoot in that ten seconds, that shot will automatically be scored as a clear miss. If your weapon hangs fire, you will be permitted to switch to another weapon which I will provide. You will be given another ten seconds to fire. If your weapon should hang fire again, you will be disqualified from the competition."

Hanging fire is something that old-fashioned black-powder weapons do occasionally. The way a black-powder weapon works, the hammer smashes a little percussion cap, which explodes, throwing a spark down a tiny hole, which in turn ignites the powder and makes the gun fire. But sometimes it just doesn't work. The spark may sit there inside the little hole, sizzling away for a several seconds, and the gun may go off unpredictably. Or it may never fire. So once a gun hangs fire, you just have to set it down in a safe place and leave it for a while.

It didn't happen often. But it was something you had to watch out for.

Colonel Taylor took his cigar out of his mouth, held it up in the air. "Ladies and gentlemen, load your weapons!"

For the first time, it hit me that I was actually *here*. I was actually competing in this thing that I'd been focused on for, what, five or six years? After everything that had happened this past week, my mind wasn't really on it, though.

Plus, what was the point? Misty would crush me anyway.

Suddenly my heart was pounding away in my chest. I was so nervous that I had this tired, almost sleepy feeling.

Misty loaded her weapon with rapid mechanical efficiency, then turned to me and frowned. "What are you doing? Load up!"

I swallowed. But it was like I couldn't move.

"Don't be a *moe*-ron!" she snapped. "Load *up*!"

Still I couldn't move.

"This is the moment," she whispered. "All these years you've been trying to break the shooter's curse. It's up to you and me. How many times have you given me the same speech about this curse, about how every year the best shooter comes in here all confident? And every year they lose to some boring Winner-and-Achiever type like Andy Davis or Garrett Rothenberg. It's time to break the curse!"

I took a deep breath. Then I removed a cartridge from my cartridge box, jammed it in the muzzle, pulled out the ramrod, and rammed it home. There was something about the motion, repeating this same physical act that I'd done thousands and thousands of times before, that calmed me a little. My pulse was still racing. But at least I was moving.

"Aim!" Colonel Taylor barked.

I was still fumbling with the percussion cap as everyone else raised their rifles. My hands were trembling and I could barely get the percussion cap seated.

"Fire!"

A ragged thunder of noise erupted as I raised my gun to aim. In front of me I searched for the target. All I could see was a cloud of white smoke. Usually there was a pretty good wind coming off the Atlantic to blow away the smoke. But today, not a breath of wind.

Where was the target? Where was the target?

I could feel the seconds ticking away.

"Five seconds," Colonel Taylor called.

And then the smoke finally started to thin out. I searched frantically. And then there it was. The target seemed to materialize out of thin air. I let the front sight settle on the target. It was jumping around with each beat of my heart. I tried to steady my pulse, but that only seemed to make things worse.

You know how to do this, I thought. After all that hundred-yard shooting, this was child's play. Even with the sight jumping around, you just took up the slack in the trigger, slowly, slowly, let your unconscious mind find the target. The ten ring seemed to swell and expand in front of me.

Pow! I fired.

"Time!" Colonel Taylor called.

Boy, I had shaved it close!

It wasn't a great shot. I could see the ragged tear on the edge of the ten ring, hanging halfway into the nine. But that was okay. Anything on the line went to the higher score. Ten. I glanced over at Misty's target. Ten, of course. Smack dead center. I scanned a couple more targets. Sevens, eights, fives. Suddenly a surge of confidence ran through me. I could *do* this. I could crush these guys!

It was just me and Misty. Nobody else even had a chance. If not me, then her. At least one of us would finally break the shooter's curse. I smiled.

"Second shot," Colonel Taylor yelled. "Load!"

I loaded quickly, my body taking over so that I didn't even have to think. I could feel my pulse slowing, all my nervousness falling away.

"Aim!"

I lifted my rifle, let the sight settle on the ten ring.

"Fire!"

I pulled the trigger. Even though a blanket of smoke now covered the target, I knew instinctively that I'd scored a ten.

The smoke cleared, revealing our targets. Misty: ten. Me: ten. The next few targets were mostly eights and nines.

"Third shot! Load!"

As I rammed the cartridge home for the third shot, something occurred to me. What if we both scored perfect 100s? It would be unprecedented. Two winners, two perfect scores. What if we both got to do it? Standing there, side by side on the stage in front of everybody? I know, I know, it was totally dorky—but just thinking about that gave me this gooshy feeling of happiness.

"Fire!"

It was so easy now. I was in the zone. Another perfect shot. Another ten.

"Fourth shot! Load!"

I could feel Misty moving beside me like my twin. We could have been on one of those Marine Corps drill teams, every movement precise and coordinated, like it was one brain for two bodies.

"Aim!"

Misty and I raised our rifles together in two perfectly matching arcs.

"Fire!"

The smoke cleared on two more tens. And in that moment I was sure that I couldn't miss. Everything she had taught me this year had suddenly emerged in my bones. *I am a monster! I am unbeatable! I can't miss!*

"Fifth shot! Load!"

It was the same now. Nothing would change. It would all be perfect. If I could just live in this moment for the rest of my life, standing next to Misty, shooting and shooting . . . oh, man! It would be the greatest. We were like a perfect machine—unstoppable, pure, clean.

"Aim!"

The ten ring was as big as all the world now. I barely even had to aim. It was as though my rifle and I were pulled toward the bull's-eye by some gravitational force, like a planet being sucked into a black hole. There was no escape from perfection.

"Fire!"

Two tens.

And so it went. Shot six. Shot seven. Shot eight . . .

I had stopped even glancing at the other targets. In fact, the only thing that I sensed about my surroundings was that between shots there was a reverent silence in the air. Everyone watching us—the faculty, the other members of the Dartington Rifles, the kids in the crowd—had perceived that something extraordinary was happening. They had stopped worrying about their own shots and were just watching us, watching something magical unfurl. It wasn't just good shooting, it was perfection. It was a moment they would remember for the rest of their lives. *I was there when Cleary and Crandall broke the shooter's curse.*

"Shot nine!" Colonel Taylor called. "Load."

I loaded. But for the first time, something seemed vaguely amiss. I couldn't put my finger on it. It wasn't anything big. Just the tiniest, most imperceptible *something.*

"Aim!"

And then the vast bull's-eye swallowed my gun sight and everything was fine again. I couldn't miss.

"Fire!"

I gently squeezed the trigger.

Nothing.

For a moment I couldn't figure it out. The front sight wobbled and weaved. And then I knew. Damn it.

"Hang fire!" I yelled.

"Raise your rifle!" Colonel Taylor yelled back.

I raised my rifle to a forty-five-degree angle. It was now pointed off toward the Barrens. Colonel Taylor counted off a full minute. Still the rifle didn't fire.

"Place your weapon in the hang-fire rack," Colonel Taylor said.

We had a special rack for hang fires. You locked the rifle in so it wouldn't fall over, the weapon aimed upward so if it fired suddenly, the bullet would drop harmlessly into the Barrens.

Colonel Taylor picked up the backup weapon, an old rifle that had probably been around back when Dad was my age. My heart sank. My own gun had been carefully sighted, adjusted, accurized . . . But this?—this was just some old piece of junk off the shelf. It would be fine for somebody like Andy Davis, who was standing there next to me blowing sevens and eights and nines. But for a ten-ring shooter? It just wasn't good enough.

As I walked to my lane, Colonel Taylor said, "It's a good rifle, son. Doesn't look like much, but I sighted it in myself. It's a shooter."

This did nothing to improve my confidence. I walked slowly to my lane and glanced over at Misty's target. She'd shot a ten, of course.

"Load!"

I loaded slowly and carefully. I must have done something wrong on the previous shot. I was determined not to do it again.

"Don't overthink it," Misty whispered. "You know how to do it. Relax."

But I couldn't. Suddenly I felt the eyes of the entire crowd on me. And my mind flashed back to the other day when Dad was arrested, all those eyes staring at me, pitying me, judging me, laughing at me.

"Aim!"

I lifted the rifle. This time the ten ring just sat there, a tiny round circle barely bigger than a pencil eraser. I let the sight settle.

Bang!

There was a murmur from the crowd. For a panicky moment I thought I'd fired before he gave the order. But no, it was my own rifle, back there on the hang-fire rack, going off by itself.

Colonel Taylor held up his hands, quieting the crowd. "That was just a hang fire!" he yelled. "Aim! Fire!"

I squeezed the trigger and the gun bucked against my arm. It was all wrong. The feel of the gun, the balance, everything.

And when the smoke cleared, of course, there it was: a nine.

Another sound from the crowd. "Ohhhhhhhh!" Everybody sounding disappointed. I felt myself deflate. Once again, I'd disappointed everybody. Once again, I'd lived up to expectations and choked.

David Crandall, appendix. David Crandall, the last of the Great Crandalls, the choker, the guy who failed to live up to—

But there was no time to sit around feeling sorry for myself. Colonel Taylor simply called out the next command. "Final shot! Load!"

I loaded, my arms feeling like wood. As I loaded I realized that Colonel Taylor was right. It *was* a nice weapon. Not pretty, but serviceable and shipshape. It would shoot where I pointed it.

So I determined to go down with dignity. Even if I didn't win, I'd finish strong. Even if Misty shot a hundred, I'd still have the third-best score in the two-hundred-and-eleven-year history of the contest. It would be better shooting than Dad, better shooting than his father, better shooting than any of the freakin' Great Crandalls had ever shot in the history of the world. Except, of course, for Elliot Crandall III, the guy who'd brought on the shooter's curse in the first place.

"Aim!"

I lifted the rifle to my shoulder. Out of the corner of my eye, I could feel Misty. Once again, we had locked into each other. I took a slow breath and smiled. It was okay. In that tiny moment, the world was perfect again.

"Fire!"

I knew the shot was perfect. Not a question in my mind.

The smoke slowly, slowly drifted and swirled and dissipated. And there it was: a ten. *All right,* I thought. *Not bad. A ninety-nine. Respectable.*

Then I looked over at Misty's target. I blinked. It couldn't be!

But it was. Her last shot had gone wide. No more than three-quarters of an inch. But wide, nevertheless. It was an eight. A clean eight. No question of it chewing up the line of the nine ring.

Misty had shot a ninety-eight. I had shot a ninety-nine.

There was no applause from the audience, no sound at all. Just stunned silence. There hadn't been a shoot-out like this in memory.

I felt a strange burst of emotion. Sadness, anger, triumph, happiness. And a wistful sense that nothing I ever did in my life after this would be quite as pure and clean and simple as what had happened here in the past fifteen minutes.

"Judges!" Colonel Taylor called. "Gather and score the targets."

I felt tears running down my face. I turned and stumbled away from the range, headed straight back toward the dorm. And then pretty soon I was running.

I ran up the stairs and into my room. Then I hurled myself on the bed and began to cry like a baby. As I lay there, I felt something in my pocket digging into my leg. It was the papers Misty and I had found. I had folded them up and jammed them in my pants. I pulled them out and threw them on the bed.

After a minute there was a soft knock on the door. I looked up and saw Misty peeking through the doorway.

I felt embarrassed. It was obvious I'd been crying.

"You threw the last shot," I said accusingly.

She didn't say anything.

"Why?"

She shrugged. "It meant something to you. You grew up here. Your dad was First Shot, your granddad was First Shot. There's all that history-of-the-Great-Crandalls crap. I just came to The Arsenal senior year so I could improve my chances of getting into an Ivy League college. What do I care if I win First Shot or not?"

"You're a *moe*-ron," I said.

She looked at me curiously. "That sounds like something I would say." Then she laughed a little. "Are you doing okay?"

"Can you just leave me alone?" I said.

Her eyes widened. "Sor*reee*!" she said. "Excuse me for caring."

I can't even tell you what was going through my mind. All I knew was I wanted to be by myself.

I jumped up, ran past her, and tore off down the hall.

• • •

I don't even know what I did the rest of the afternoon. Wandered around the Barrens a little. Went down to the rocky beach over on the other side of the Point. Wandered around campus. Just wandered and wandered.

Finally I started getting hungry. I went into the dining hall, got my food, and sat down at a table by myself.

Other than graduation, school was pretty much finished, so most of the underclassmen had already started filtering away. The dining hall was nearly empty. Like the brochure said—"bleak and cheerless" were the exact right words to describe it.

Suddenly I had a terrible thought. The papers! I'd left them on my bed.

I sprinted to my room.

The door was open. And the papers were gone.

30

I started tearing the room apart. But I knew exactly where I'd left them. Sitting out in plain view on the bed.

What had I been thinking?

No doubt one of Mr. Rothenberg's thugs had come by and snagged them off the bed. And now Mr. Rothenberg was sitting around laughing his butt off about how stupid I'd been. Then I heard somebody behind me, clearing their throat. I whirled around.

It was Garrett Rothenberg.

"So . . ." he said. He had a funny look on his face. Not his usual smirky, cocky expression. "You okay?"

"Gee," I said, "why shouldn't I be?"

He sat down heavily on the bed. "Man, I just had the hugest fight with my dad."

"Yeah?" I said, not really interested.

"I mean, what's up with him? Everything I've achieved and it's never enough." He shook his head. "I almost wish I hadn't won."

"Won what?" I said.

Rothenberg didn't answer me. Which was typical. He wasn't exactly what you'd call a *good listener*. "Can I ask you a question?" Rothenberg said.

I shrugged.

"When you go to bed every day, do you think, *God, I was such a jerk today?*"

I frowned, thinking. "No," I said. "Not really."

"Because, like, every day when I go to bed I just think what an asshole I am. You know? Kids I made fun of, people I messed with, lies I told, stuff I did that made people feel bad. And for what?"

"I don't know, Rothenberg," I said. "And, honestly, I don't give a crap."

He laughed loudly, this time like what I said was really funny. "I bet you don't," he said. "After I took the one thing away from you that matters in your life."

"What?" I said. "You took those papers?"

"Papers?" He frowned.

"There were some papers—" I broke off. What was the point? So he'd had a little fight with his dad and now he was Mr. Sensitive for three minutes. I didn't think it would be a red-hot idea to get into the whole thing about his dad and the papers I'd stupidly left on the bed.

"Nah," he said. "I was talking about this afternoon."

I frowned. "What happened this afternoon?"

He looked curiously at me. "You know . . . when I won."

"Seriously," I said. "What did you win?"

He blinked. "Uh . . ." he said. Suddenly his eye widened. "Are you telling me you didn't know?"

"Know *what*?" I was kind of starting to get irritated with him.

Garrett Rothenberg looked up at me. "You didn't know?" he said. "I won."

"Won *what*?"

He cleared his throat, sat down on the bed. "All those afternoons when I said I was going to tennis lessons? Actually I was taking shooting lessons. The top shooting coach in America lives over in Lewiston. What a coincidence, huh?"

My mind was blank, uncomprehending. "I don't understand."

"It was my dad's idea. He can't stand the idea of a Rothenberg losing. At anything."

I squinted at him.

"Ten tens," Rothenberg said. "I shot ten tens. I won. I'm First Shot."

For a minute I thought he was joking. I started to laugh.

But he just looked at me, blank-faced. Then I realized, hey, I'd walked away from the contest before they'd even finished scoring it. And Garrett had been in the shooting lane at the far end of the range. Too far for me to see his target while I was shooting.

"Ten tens?" I said quietly.

He nodded. "My rifle cost almost twenty grand. I've had it all year and it's never hung fire, not once. If you'd had my rifle, we'd have tied."

For a second I felt sick. Then I felt something bitter and angry welling up in the middle of my chest. What was it about Garrett? No matter what I did, he could always make me feel small.

Garrett sighed loudly. "I wish you'd won," he said. "It actually *meant* something to you. To me it was just . . . something to get my old man off my back. I *hate* shooting. The smell of the smoke, the sound of the gun, the—" He broke off, his face twisted with disgust. "I hate this school. I hate my dad. I hate myself. I hate everything."

I want to scream at him, hit him, do *something* to hurt him. But instead I just sat there like a lump.

"What is it with parents?" he said. He sat there for a long time, staring up in the air. "I used to think my dad was the greatest guy in the world, you know? I thought he was the smartest guy, the strongest guy, the best tennis player, the funniest guy, the coolest . . ." He laughed, but not with any humor. "Then you finally start to get it. Your dad's actually a big schmuck who's putting on a front."

"I don't know," I said. "I thought that for a while about my dad. But not anymore."

He frowned. "I mean . . . your dad . . . um . . ." He looked embarrassed. "He . . . killed . . . your mom. Right?"

I shook my head. "No. Actually, not. He didn't do it."

Rothenberg looked like he thought I was total idiot, like maybe I'd gone to see Dad in jail and Dad had somehow convinced me he didn't do it. Which is kind of the opposite of what actually happened.

"So who did?" he said.

This whole situation was totally bizarre and uncomfortable. Here I was having this conversation with this guy whose dad had done something terrible to my mother, who'd framed my dad, who'd—

"It doesn't matter," I said. "Without the papers, I can't prove anything."

"Papers?" he said. "What are these papers you keep babbling about?"

"I left some papers on my bed . . . " I waved my hand, flicking away the question. "Hey, it doesn't even matter."

Rothenberg stared at me for a long time. "Can I tell you something really weird?" he said finally.

"Whatever, man," I said.

"I don't mean this to sound all gay or whatever. But I always admired you."

"Me?" Who was he kidding?

"Seriously." He was staring straight at me, not a shred of irony on his face. "The whole time I've known you, you've always done your own thing. Scribbling your little stories in your notebooks, going out there and shooting all the time, goofing off in the classes you don't care about. I totally respect that."

"That's nice."

A brief spark of anger flashed in his eyes. "I'm serious, dude. Did you know . . . " He hesitated. "Did you know I used to snoop around in your stuff?"

"No duh," I said. "Why do you think I passworded my computer first semester?"

"You *knew*?"

"I'm not an idiot."

He cleared his throat. "Well, it's not exactly like it sounds. What happened was, my dad set it up so that I'd be your roommate. He told me he wanted me to keep an eye on you."

"Why?"

"He didn't say."

"You're telling me your father told you to *spy* on another kid? And it never occurred to you to ask why?"

Rothenberg looked exasperated. "Dude, I'm making a point here! Okay? The point I'm making is, he wanted me to snoop on you. So I did. I read your notebooks. I read your e-mail. At first I was just checking up on you, doing what Dad said. But then, after a while, I started . . ." He flushed. "After a while, I started liking it."

I couldn't figure out what he was talking about. And the truth is, I didn't care. "Is that why we got chased around in the tunnels?" I said. "You told your dad that I had some weird old key and was going to go down into the tunnels? And he sent somebody after us?"

"Dude, I'm talking," he said. Then he picked up the train of his thought again: "I mean, like, when I read your stories, it was like, *This guy actually has an original thought in his head every now and then!* I mean, I couldn't write stories like that in a million years. Never. And in your e-mails? You were always, like . . . *nice* to people. I just felt so envious. It was like . . ."

"What?"

He looked at the floor. His voice came out hushed and sheepish-sounding. "It was like . . . I wanted to be like you."

"Great." I couldn't think of anything more preposterous.

"Even Misty. When I saw you liked her, I said to myself, *Okay, I'm gonna have her.* Just because Crandall digs her."

I got up and punched him in the middle of his face. Three times. As hard as I could.

He grabbed hold of his nose, curled up in a ball on the bed, didn't even try to defend himself. Then I sat back down and watched the blood leak out of his fingers. And I didn't feel one bit bad about it.

"How's that for nice?" I said finally.

After a minute, he took one hand away from his face. He reached into his back pocket, pulled something out, and threw it on the bed.

A stack of folded papers.

"My dad told me to snoop around, look for them," he said.

I grabbed them off the bed. They were the papers I'd

been looking for. They were lightly smeared with blood from Rothenberg's nose. I knew I had to get the papers out of there or his dad would show up with his goons and take them from me. I also knew I had to find somebody who could make sense of them, explain what they meant. Because they didn't mean squat to me. And then after that I'd have to get them to Chief Dowd.

"I hate my dad," Rothenberg said. His voice sounded all goofy because of having a bashed-in nose. "I hate him so much."

"Thanks, Rothenberg," I said, waving the papers at him. Then I headed for the hallway. I stopped at the door, looked back into my room, and said, "Oh, hey, and congratulations on winning First Shot. Ten tens? That's some great shooting."

He looked up at me, eyes full self-loathing. "Screw you, Crandall," he said. "Why do you have to be so nice?"

I ran down the stairs and out the front door of the dorm, not even quite sure where I was going. But just sure that I needed to get those papers hidden somewhere.

I was so busy thinking about the papers that I didn't see the man stepping out in front of me as I blew through the front door.

WHAM!

I smashed into the man, and then fell down on the ground. Above me stood a short bald guy in a dark suit. I felt like I'd just hit a brick wall. The man didn't seem to have been the slightest bit affected by my smashing into him. He was built like a fireplug.

"Sorry," I said.

I looked at the man's face and suddenly I had the terrible thought that maybe this was another one of Mr. Rothenberg's thugs. He had a face like one of these UFC martial arts guys, like somebody who'd had his nose broken a few times, maybe been elbowed in the face quite a few times.

I tried to get up, but I'd pretty well had the breath knocked out of me. The short fireplug of a man reached out toward me. I still had the papers in my hand.

"No!" I said.

He looked down at me with an amused expression.

Somebody else came around the corner. A shadow fell across my legs. For a second I thought sure it was going to be Mr. Rothenberg again.

But it wasn't.

I looked up and there was Misty standing over me.

"Oh," she said. "Hi, David. I see you've met my dad."

31

The first thing I thought when I saw Misty's dad was: *How did this funny-looking little bald guy have such a beautiful daughter?* They didn't seem to look at all alike.

Misty's dad grinned, grabbed my arm, and hoisted me to my feet. He looked like a chubby little guy, but he was incredibly strong.

"Oh!" he said. "So you're this David Crandall we've been hearing so much about. Sounds like you're in a little bit of a hole right now, kid." Like Misty, he had a strong Southern accent.

I nodded. I was still having trouble catching my breath after slamming into him.

"Have you still got those papers?" Misty said. "Maybe Dad could take a look at them."

I handed them mutely to Mr. Cleary. He glanced at Misty. "Man of few words, huh?"

"Sorry," I said. "Kind of knocked the breath out of me."

Mr. Cleary examined the papers, which had now been

folded and refolded about eight times and were starting to look a little the worse for wear. He frowned, squinted at the pages, and nodded sagely. "Yep," he said. "I know exactly what these are."

I waited with anticipation.

"These," he said, holding the papers up, "are pieces of paper with numbers on them."

Misty slapped his arm. "You are such a *jerk*!"

Mr. Cleary laughed. "You got a minute, David?" he said. "Truth is, all I know about money is that I've never got enough of the dadgum stuff. Maybe we can let Misty's mom take a look at them."

"Sure," I said. I looked around nervously. I was afraid Mr. Rothenberg and his thugs might show up any minute. "But I don't want to drag you into my problems. I don't know how much Misty told you about—"

He waved his hand dismissively. "Hey, don't even sweat it. Nobody's gonna mess with you in broad daylight. Not when you're with us, anyway."

"Oh," I said. "Okay."

"Misty's mother used to be a banker," Mr. Cleary said, handing the papers back to me. "She knows all about this kind of junk."

As he was saying that, an SUV pulled up at the curb in front of the dorm and a tall, elegant woman climbed out. *Now* I saw where Misty had gotten her genes from. She almost could have been Misty, twenty-five years from now.

She waved at us and we all walked over to the car, where Misty introduced us.

She had Misty's features, but her eyes were blue and her hair was darker, with a long gray streak over one ear. Unlike Misty's jolly father, she also had Misty's coolness and reserve.

"Hop in, David," Mr. Cleary said. "I'm starving. We'll take a look at these papers of yours while we get some chow."

"Wow, okay," I said. I climbed in the backseat next to Misty.

"What'll it be?" her dad said. "Steak? Seafood? French cuisine? Chinese?"

"Uh, I believe there's only one restaurant in Dartington," Misty said.

"I knew that!" Mr. Cleary said, winking at me in the rearview mirror. Then he turned to his wife. "Hon, how about taking a look at David's mysterious papers. Maybe you can shed a little light on what's going on here."

I passed the papers up to her. "Hm," she said. Then she flipped around a little more, frowning with concentration. It was uncanny: she looked exactly like Misty did when she was shooting—the same focus, the same little line forming between her brows and everything.

Suddenly I noticed Mr. Cleary looking at me in the rearview mirror. He grinned. "I know what you're thinking."

"Excuse me?" I said.

"You're wondering if Misty inherited anything from me at all. Other than my good looks, of course." He laughed.

"Well . . ." I said.

"Misty's mom can't shoot worth a hoot," he said. "In fact, she gets all weird and googly-eyed if you even *show* her a gun."

"Roger," Misty's mom said coolly, "I'm concentrating. Maybe you could knock off the comedy routine until I'm done?"

"Yes, ma'am," Mr. Cleary said. He seemed like he was half joking . . . and half scared of her.

We had almost gotten to the village when Mr. Cleary's cell phone rang. He answered and then said, "How did you get this number?" Suddenly his voice didn't sound very humorous at all. After a few seconds he took the phone away from his ear and looked at it carefully. Then he handed it back to me. "It's for you," he said.

"Hello?"

"Hi there, David," a man's voice said. I didn't recognize it. "I'm going to put a friend of yours on."

There were a couple of thumps and bumps. Then a voice came on the phone.

"Davy? Is that you?" It was Leo. He sounded scared. My heart sank. I knew immediately where this was going.

"Are you okay?" I said. But I knew he wasn't.

"Look, they want me to . . ." There was a thump and a grunt. "Don't do anything they say!" Leo shouted.

And that was all he said. There was another thump and then a cry of pain. "Leo? Leo?"

The man's voice came back on. "Your friend is with us," he said. "You need to give him a hand because he's in kind of a jam. If you see what I'm getting at."

My voice came out weak and high-sounding: "Do you work for Mr. Rothenberg or—"

"Shut up, kid," the voice said. "I'm talking. Bring the papers to Leo's trailer. Don't discuss this with anyone. Talk to the cops, and Leo will not make it through the night. On the other hand, you bring the papers, you cooperate, you act smart . . . and Leo will live a long and happy life."

I had this terrible sick feeling in my chest. "But . . ."

"I said shut up. Be at the trailer park in fifteen minutes."

The phone went dead. I literally felt like I was about to throw up.

"Uh . . ." I said softly. "I have to do something."

I handed the phone back to Mr. Cleary. "What's going on?" Mr. Cleary said.

"That was . . . a friend of mine. He needed me to, um, do something for him."

"How did he get my phone number?" There was no joking around in Mr. Cleary's manner.

"I don't know." I cleared my throat. "Could I, uh, have my papers back?"

"I'm not sure that's a good idea," Mrs. Cleary said. "These are very disturbing."

I could see the trailer park where the Jackstaffs all lived coming up on the right. "Could you kinda pull over here?"

"What's going on?" Mr. Cleary said.

"My friend Leo," I said. "They have my friend Leo."

"Who does? This Rothenberg guy?"

I nodded.

Mr. Cleary blew by the trailer park, didn't even slow down.

"Sir?" I said. "I really need to . . ."

"How long have you got?" he said.

"Fifteen minutes."

"Mm-kay," he said. "Let's try something." He pulled out his phone and dialed a number.

"Please!" I said.

"Just trust me for a minute," he said. "This is what I do."

I looked over at Misty. She nodded at me. "It *is* what he does."

Somehow this didn't comfort me.

"Bobby," Mr. Cleary said. "It's Roger. I need help and I need it fast. I want you to give me a location on a man by the name of Rothenberg. I need you to triangulate his location from his cell-phone signal." He put his hand over the phone, looked back at me. "What's his first name?"

"John."

"John Rothenberg. He's a partner in a firm called Rothenberg, Lyttle. Right? Rothenberg, Lyttle?"

I nodded.

"Uh-huh. Uh-huh. Uh-huh. Nope. No, I'm staying on the line." Mr. Cleary looked in the mirror at me again. "The best defense is a good offense, huh?"

"Look—"

He held up his finger, cutting me off. "My amigo," he said into the phone, "you are the best. Put this one on my tab."

He put the phone on the dash and hung a U-turn.

"Where are we going?"

"To have a little chat with your friend Mr. John Rothenberg."

"But . . ."

"Trust me."

He turned to Mrs. Cleary. "Give me the bullet points. I need to know what's in those papers."

Five minutes later, we were zooming into the front gate of The Arsenal. Mr. Cleary drove through campus. Parked along the curb were several black limousines. Mr. Cleary passed them, then bumped up over the curve and drove right across the grass of the quad.

"Four-wheelin'!" Mr. Cleary said. "Gotta love it."

He skidded to a stop right in front of Crandall House, hopped out. "Come with me, son," he said. "Misty, you and your mama stay in the car."

I followed him as he bounded up the stairs. He ran through the front door.

"You know where the boardroom is?" he said.

I pointed at the stairs. For a short chubby guy, he sure moved fast. I followed him up the stairs, my heart pounding. What was he *doing*?

At the top of the stairs was a pair of huge mahogany doors. "There," I said.

Mr. Cleary threw open the doors. We walked into the room where the board of directors of The Arsenal met. It was paneled in dark wood and there were pictures of a lot of old guys hanging on the walls—some of them my ancestors.

A very large table filled most of the room. Seated around the table were a bunch of men and women in suits. Mr. Rothenberg sat at the head of the table. He was saying something and everybody around the table was laughing.

He broke off and glanced at me and Mr. Cleary. Everybody stopped laughing.

Mr. Cleary looked around the room. "Who's Rothenberg?" he shouted. No more jolly Mr. Cleary. He seemed to be able to turn jolly Mr. Cleary off and on. Now he was scary Mr. Cleary. There was something about him, an aura of command, that just came off him in waves.

All the members of the board were looking really uncomfortable all of a sudden.

Mr. Rothenberg smiled thinly. "Sir, I don't know who you are, nor do I care, but you've just interrupted a meeting of the board of directors. I'd appreciate your leaving right now." Mr. Rothenberg had that aura-of-command thing pretty well down himself.

Mr. Cleary looked around the room. "Everybody out. Now."

Mr. Rothenberg pulled out his cell phone, hit one button. "Guys," he said. "We've got a situation."

"Now!" Mr. Cleary said.

The members of the board were looking kind of shell-shocked. They didn't have to be asked again. Whatever was going on, they didn't want to be part of it. They all filed quickly out the door. Mr. Cleary grabbed me by the arm and propelled me around the table so that we were facing the doors.

I could hear footsteps thundering up the stairs—undoubtedly Mr. Rothenberg's security guards.

Mr. Cleary waited until two large men in suits appeared at the door.

"Shut the door, boys," Mr. Cleary ordered them.

"Who are you?" the larger of the two men said.

"I told you to shut the door." Mr. Cleary's black eyes stared at them like laser beams.

The two men looked nervously at Mr. Rothenberg. Mr. Rothenberg nodded slightly. As soon as the doors were closed, both men pulled out pistols and pointed them at Mr. Cleary.

I felt woozy and weak in the knees, so I sat down in one of the big leather chairs.

"Who are you?" Mr. Rothenberg said. "And what do you want?"

"My name is Roger Cleary," Mr. Cleary said. "I'm the president of ISI Security Corporation. I have been retained by Mr. Crandall here." For a second I thought he was talking about my dad. But then I realized he was talking about me. "The papers you are seeking to recover have been turned over to a forensic accountant and analyzed. In summary, they describe a scheme to defraud The Arsenal of approximately twenty-four point six million dollars, a fraud committed by you, which you managed to blame on the former headmaster of The Arsenal, Dr. Grantland Boyce. The papers have been duplicated and will be turned over to the Federal Bureau of Investigation. You have thirty seconds to make the call to your people and release Leo Jackstaff."

"Or what?" Mr. Rothenberg said. I have to give the guy credit. He seemed pretty calm about the whole thing.

"Mr. Rothenberg, kidnapping is a federal crime punishable by life imprisonment in a federal correctional facility."

Mr. Rothenberg shrugged. "I just don't have a clue what you're talking about."

Mr. Cleary folded his arms. "Make the call."

"I don't know what you're talking about."

"All right, fair enough," Mr. Cleary said. "We've got the papers. Come on, David, let's get out of here."

"Look," Mr. Rothenberg said, "I'm still confused about what you want, but before anybody goes off half-cocked, let's sit down and have a conversation."

Mr. Cleary smiled. "I thought so," he said. Then he sat down next to me. "Before we talk, though, tell those *moe*-rons to put their guns away."

"If we're going to have a frank conversation," Mr. Rothenberg said, "then I'll need to make sure that you aren't wired."

"Fair enough," Mr. Cleary said.

Mr. Rothenberg turned to his guards. "Sweep them."

One of the big guards came over, took some kind of black electronic device out of his coat pocket, and ran it over Mr. Cleary, then over me—up our legs, across our bodies, up and down our arms. "Turn off the cell phone, please, sir," the guard said.

Mr. Cleary nodded, turned off his cell phone, and set it on the table.

The guard passed the device across the cell phone, then nodded to Mr. Rothenberg.

"Step outside," Mr. Rothenberg said to his guards. "Make sure nobody comes in."

We waited until the two big men were gone.

Mr. Rothenberg looked at me. "Jesus, kid. You are one serious pain in the neck."

"Talk to me," Mr. Cleary said.

"Cleary?" Mr. Rothenberg said. "You wouldn't happen to be Garrett's little girlfriend's father, would you?"

"*Former* girlfriend," Mr. Cleary said. "My impression, she's a lot more interested in David here." He smiled. "But, hey, what do I know about women?"

Mr. Rothenberg spread his hands. "You have the papers. But you know what? David's dad is still in jail. Still charged with quite a terrible crime. I admit these papers are pretty damn embarrassing to me. But they won't get the kid's dad out of jail. I mean, the guy confessed."

Mr. Cleary said, "Point taken. Let's reduce the elements of this conversation, huh? Make the call. Let this kid Leo go."

Mr. Rothenberg shrugged, made a brief call. "Done," he said.

"Good."

"Here's the thing," Mr. Rothenberg said. "I had nothing to do with David's mom's murder. That's a fact. These papers have nothing to do with that."

"She found the papers," I said. "They must have been in that old safe. Once she figured out what was going on, she was going to go to the police. You found out. And you had her killed."

"Good story," Mr. Rothenberg said. "Unfortunately, not true."

"Tell us another story, then," Mr. Cleary said.

"That little punk Nolan Jackstaff found them. He took

them to David's mother because she worked in the accounting department at the school. She quickly figured out what had happened. She wanted to go to the police. But Nolan said no. He had a better idea."

"Which was what?" I said.

"Nolan called me up on the phone, said, 'Hey, Mr. Rothenberg, I got something you might want.' Then he asked for thirty thousand dollars."

"What did you do?" I said.

Mr. Rothenberg laughed. "The kid was trailer trash," he said derisively. "Didn't have a clue what this stuff was worth. I'd have paid him ten times that. Are you kidding? I sent one of my guys up, gave him the thirty grand, he gave me the papers . . . and then my guy beat the hell out of the kid."

There was a long silence in the room.

"Nolan wasn't as dumb as you think," I said finally. "He made copies."

"He made copies," Mr. Rothenberg said. "He sure did. Hit me up for another thirty grand about two weeks later. Said it was to pay for Band-Aids."

"What does this have to do with my mom?" I said.

"That's my point," Mr. Rothenberg said. "It has nothing to do with your mom. Two weeks after I paid the kid another thirty grand, he got arrested on a drug conviction. And off he went to the state pen. That's the last time I ever heard from him."

"But . . . "

Mr. Rothenberg laughed sourly. "You can ask a million questions, David. We can sit here all day. But I had jack to do with your mother's death."

I looked at Mr. Cleary. He looked back at me expressionlessly.

"Here's the thing, pal," Mr. Rothenberg said to me. "I don't think your dad killed your mom. I've known him for a while. It's not in him. Based on the conversation I had with Garrett about five minutes ago, it sounds like whoever shot your mother also framed your father. Assuming that he did not, in fact, kill your mother, it sounds like your father confessed because he believed you did it and wanted to keep you from going to jail. But now that he's confessed, well, that puts him in quite a predicament. It's gonna take a whole *mountain* of evidence to get him off. And some seriously good lawyering."

"What's that got to do with anything?" I said.

"A top-quality defense in a homicide case costs money— truly ridiculous amounts of money. O. J. Simpson spent over ten million dollars on his trial. I'm guessing your dad—selfless pedagogue that he is—does not have that kind of money."

"What are you proposing?" Mr. Cleary said.

"A million dollars. I'll budget a million bucks for lawyers, investigators, you name it. On two conditions."

"And those are . . ."

"One, I get the papers back. All of them. Two, in the course of defending your father, nobody ever mentions these papers. Or this little scheme I was . . . ah . . . *allegedly* involved in."

"Hold on," I said. "Look, I'm not a financial genius or whatever. But what exactly was this scheme that you did?"

"I used the word *allegedly,* did you notice that? I'm not admitting to anything."

"Hey!" I said. "I may be a kid, but I'm not stupid."

Mr. Cleary jumped in and said, "David is right. You swept the room. There's nothing being recorded here. You want a frank conversation? Okay, be frank."

Mr. Rothenberg cleared his throat. "All right. Look, hey, the whole business happened kind of by accident. Back when your mother's father, Grantland Boyce, was the headmaster, I was a young financial manager. I was an Arsenal grad and I talked him into letting me manage the school's investments. I ran into some financial problems at my firm and I kind of, uh, dipped into The Arsenal funds. My intention was to pay them back. But it just wasn't possible. Ultimately Dr. Boyce found out I'd taken the money. It looked like it would destroy The Arsenal. Dr. Boyce felt personally responsible. After all, he'd hired me. And frankly, he hadn't paid nearly as much attention to what I was doing as he should have.

"So anyway," he went on, "a little face-saving compromise was worked out between me, Dr. Boyce, and the board of directors. Well, mainly it was worked out between me and Boyce. See, The Arsenal was Dr. Boyce's whole life. If it failed, then he would have felt like he'd pretty much wasted his whole life. I understood that about him. So I used it against him. I said that if he'd do what I told him, I'd save the school for him."

"What did you tell him to do?" I said.

"I told him to go to the board of directors and tell them that he'd stolen the money. Could he have proved what I'd done, showed them that he was innocent? Of course. That's why he gathered all those papers and hid them in that safe. But if he had . . . it would have all gone public at that point. And most likely it would have destroyed the school. Dr. Boyce didn't want that. So he resigned. Quietly. Your dad was then appointed headmaster. It took your dad and me about five years, but we finally got the school's money situation straightened out. And, in fact, the school is now in far better financial condition than it was when Dr. Boyce ran the show here." He smiled the same cheesy smile that Garrett was always flashing at everybody. "So. All's well that ends well."

"Except that my grandfather was so ashamed about it that he killed himself."

Mr. Rothenberg shrugged, looking completely unconcerned. "Hey, nobody ever told him to off himself. He could still be down in Florida playing golf. That was his decision." He rapped one hand on the tabletop. "Deal's on the table.

Are you in or out? A million-dollar legal fund for dear old Dad—in exchange for the papers."

"Wait a second," I said. "How did the safe end up in the tunnels?"

Mr. Rothenberg swatted the air with his hand. "Who cares? It was a worn-out old safe sitting down in some gloomy old room at the end of one of the tunnels. Nobody knew there was anything important in it. I would imagine when they sealed up the tunnels, it was sitting there, too heavy to move, so they just left it in there and welded the door shut. My guess is they left the keys sitting right there on top of it. Nolan is poking around down there one day, he finds the safe, he grabs the keys, opens it up. There are the papers lying there where Dr. Boyce left them a decade earlier." He looked at his watch. "But, again—who cares? Water under the bridge. A million bucks for the papers. In or out?"

"Ten million," Mr. Cleary said.

"Two."

"Ten."

Mr. Rothenberg met Mr. Cleary's gaze. "Four. Final offer. Not a nickel more."

"Give us a minute," Mr. Cleary said.

Mr. Rothenberg gave him a long, cold stare, then said, "Maybe I'll go stretch my legs."

Then he left the room.

Mr. Cleary turned to me and said, "I don't know, son.

His story seems plausible. But it could be a big fat lie. Hard to know. But it raises a real question: If Nolan was the one who was blackmailing him, then why would Rothenberg want to kill your *mother*? Why not kill Nolan?"

"Maybe Mom wanted to go to the police. Maybe Mr. Rothenberg wanted to stop her."

"Maybe." Mr. Cleary made a tent of his fingers and said, "The bottom line is, we just don't have enough information to know."

"But if he didn't kill Mom, then who did?"

Mr. Cleary shook his head. "Maybe it was this Nolan kid."

"Yeah, but why? He didn't have any reason to do it."

"I don't know what to tell you."

"I think I need to talk to my dad."

Mr. Cleary nodded. "I think you're right. We need to check on your friend Leo, too, make sure he's all right."

I nodded.

"Let's roll," Mr. Cleary said.

We walked out the double doors into the hallway. Mr. Rothenberg was standing outside, talking on his cell phone. As soon as he saw me, he took his hand away from the phone. "Well?"

"I have to talk to my dad," I said.

"Deal's on the table for one hour," he said. Then he turned away from me like he had more important things to worry about.

. . .

We reached the trailer park in five minutes. "Girls, y'all stay here," Mr. Cleary said. "Me and David'll go check on him."

As I climbed out, Misty got out of the SUV, too.

"Where are *you* going?" Mr. Cleary said.

Misty didn't say anything. She just stood there with her jaw clenched, her arms crossed, and her face blank. She looked around at the collection of squalid trailers like she hadn't even heard her father.

"In the car, young lady!" Mr. Cleary said.

Misty didn't move.

"Lord have mercy," Mr. Cleary said, "she's got a head as hard as a ten-day-old biscuit." Then suddenly he had a pistol in his hand. *Okay,* I thought, *he's not fooling around.*

"It's this way," I said.

"I'm gonna go around the other way," Misty said.

"Young lady, you get back here right now!" Mr. Cleary called. But she just walked into the woods and disappeared. Mr. Cleary sighed loudly. "Can't tell her anything."

We threaded our way through the trees, eventually coming out into the weedy little clearing where Leo's trailer sat.

"You stay here," Mr. Cleary said. "I'll make sure everything's clear."

But I ignored him. I didn't want Mr. Cleary getting hurt

because of me. So I just ran over and banged on the door. "Leo!" I called. "It's me."

The door opened and Leo looked out.

"Are you okay?" I said.

He nodded. "Come on in," he said.

"That's okay," I said. "I just wanted to make sure you were okay."

I flashed a thumbs-up to Mr. Cleary. He holstered his pistol.

"Seriously," Leo said. "There's something I need to tell you."

"I'm kind of in the middle of something," I said.

Leo looked at me with this funny expression. Like I was letting him down.

"Okay," I said. "Just for a sec." I called to Mr. Cleary, "I'll be out to the car in a second."

We went over and sat down. He put his hands between his legs and squeezed them together. He seemed really nervous about something.

"What is it?" I said.

"There's something I just found out," he said.

"What's that?"

"Before Nolan died, he told me something."

"What?"

"There was a guy out there with your mom. Nolan said that when he was out in the Barrens, he saw them together," he said.

"I thought Nolan was in a coma there at the end," I said.

"Well . . . he kind of drifted in and out." Leo paused. He was blinking his eyes in a very strange way.

"Is there something wrong with your eyes?"

He stopped blinking. "Just allergies. So anyway, the first time he saw your mom, she was with this guy. Then he saw her again. And she was dead."

"What guy?"

"Some guy from The Arsenal."

"Like a kid?"

"No. I forget his name. It was like the name of somebody in one of those old rock bands, Led Zeppelin or the Rolling Stones."

"Mr. Entwhistle? The bass player for the Who was named Entwistle."

"That's right. John Entwistle." Leo's voice seemed leaden and tired.

I thought about it. Mr. Entwhistle. Why would he have been out in the Barrens with her at that time of night? It was hard to explain. And why didn't Leo mention this earlier?

"Did he have a rifle? I mean . . . was there anything else you forgot to mention here?"

"Look, last time we talked, I was pretty shook up!" Leo said.

"So shook up you forgot to mention that Mr. Entwhistle might have killed my mom?"

He sighed loudly. "I didn't want to say anything."

"Why not?"

Leo stared at one of his sneakers for a long time, bobbing his foot up and down.

"Why not?" I repeated.

"Look." His voice got so low I almost couldn't understand him. "Nolan was modeling for her. In all these pictures, right? So he was over at your house a lot. And he thought that . . ."

"That *what*?"

"That maybe your mom was having an affair with this Entwhistle guy."

"Mr. *Entwhistle*? He's like a million years old."

Leo shrugged. "I don't know about that. I'm just telling you what he said."

I sat in silence. Mr. Entwhistle and my mom? The whole idea was ridiculous. Nolan and Mom—that was distantly plausible. Nolan and Mr. Entwhistle?—no way, José.

"Look," Leo said. "Did you make copies of that stuff? Those papers you found?"

"Why?" I said.

"I've about had enough of this whole thing. Those two guys busted in here, they taped me to a chair." Leo's eyes looked a little watery. "I thought they were gonna *kill* me."

"I'm sorry," I said. "I didn't mean to drag you into this."

"I just want this to be over. If you keep copies, somewhere along the way something else will happen. And then . . . I just don't want anything to do with this guy Rothenberg again. He scares the crap out of me."

"I didn't make copies."

"So you're gonna make the trade. You give him the stuff, he gives you . . . whatever he's giving you? And it's over?"

I nodded. "It's over."

He slumped forward, put his head in his hands, then said something.

"What?" I said.

He didn't move. But something came out of his lips, very, very quiet. I still couldn't hear him.

"What?"

He sat up sharply. "Hey, look, I know you got a lot of stuff to do. . . ." Then he put his hand on my shoulder. We walked to the door. "See ya," he said. Then his voice dropped so low that I could barely hear him. "I'm sorry," he whispered, his voice so low I could hardly make it out. What was going on here? The whole time I'd been sitting with him, I'd felt like something screwy was happening. But I couldn't quite figure out what it was.

"Sorry for what?" I was feeling really puzzled now.

"You better go," he said loudly. Then he kind of shoved me out the door. I stumbled down the concrete steps to the ground and he slammed the door behind me.

"Everything okay?" Mr. Cleary said.

"I don't know. I guess." My mind was still in a whirl. My mom and Mr. Entwhistle? Having an affair? That was ridiculous.

"Good. Then let's go talk to your dad," Mr. Cleary said.

• • •

The county seat of Devonshire County is a town called Tottness. It was about twenty minutes from the village. We made it in twelve. Mr. Cleary must have been a race-car driver in his spare time, because, man, he could sure make that car move.

A few minutes later I was talking to Dad. We were sitting in a concrete-block room with white walls. Dad sat on one side of a steel table, and I sat on the other. His hands were cuffed to a steel ring on the edge of the table. He looked somehow smaller than normal. Like he'd just shrunk about six inches in the past day.

"I don't know how you can forgive me," he said. "I don't know how I could have believed it was you."

I felt a burst of anger. But the fact was, I'd done exactly the same thing, believed exactly the same thing about him. "Forget it," I said brusquely. "We've got a situation here." I explained about Mr. Rothenberg's proposition. Then I told Dad about what Leo had just told me, that Mom had been seen with Mr. Entwhistle just before she was shot.

"Entwhistle. Martin Entwhistle?" He looked off distantly for a minute. Then he said, "There are only three people who have passkeys that will open all the doors on campus. One is me. One is Bob Carruth, the maintenance supervisor. And one is Martin Entwhistle."

My eyes widened.

"He could have done it," Dad said. "I mean . . . in theory. He could have snuck in and stolen my rifle, gone to the Barrens, shot her, brought it back, put it up."

"But *why?*"

"I don't know." Dad sat for a while, looking thoughtful. Finally he said, "She confided in him. After your grandfather died, he kind of came into her life and helped guide her. In fact, I think that he did a lot to steady her, make her life easier. Maybe that's how he found out about the papers. You know, he was one of those guys who seemed like he had a really brilliant future once. He attended The Arsenal, then went to Yale, looked like the sky was the limit. Politics, law, anything. Next thing you know, he's sixty years old, no money in the bank, working for a little second-tier prep school in some jerkwater part of New England. No kids, no money, no trophies on the wall. Nothing to show for his life."

I could hear other prisoners in the distance, shouting insults at one another.

"Maybe your mother told him about those papers. And maybe he just decided, *You know what? I'm just going to cash in.* Maybe your mother said, no, we're going to burn them. Or we're going to give them to the FBI. Or whatever. So he tried to get her to give him the papers. And she refused." He sat silently for a while. "And maybe he just refused to take no for an answer."

"Is that how you feel?" I said quietly.

"What?"

"What you said about Mr. Entwhistle. You think you've got nothing to show for your life?"

He smiled sadly at me. "Right at this exact minute?" Dad said. "Yeah, I kind of feel like I've undershot the mark a little."

"No, but I mean . . ."

"I know what you mean." The sad smile faded. "I don't know. I never set out to be the man I am today, no."

"You're a great headmaster," I said. "Look at all the stuff you've done with the school. The new field house. The computer center. Saving the finances of the school. Think of all the lives you've touched, all the kids who'll look back and say how important The Arsenal was in their lives."

"Are you one of those kids?" he said.

I thought about it for a while. "In a totally weird way?" I said finally. "Yeah. I guess I am."

A door clanged somewhere back in the Devonshire County jail, then a burst of raucous laughter echoed through concrete corridors of the jail.

"What about the deal?" I said. "Should we give Mr. Rothenberg the papers? Take his money?"

"Those papers are part of my defense. If Martin Entwhistle did it, then we'll need those papers to prove it."

"So what do I tell him?"

Dad didn't move for a minute. Then he sat up very straight. Suddenly he was like the father I'd known before Mom died—tough but fair, somebody you couldn't push around if you tried. "Go tell John Rothenberg he can stuff it."

32

When I got out to the Clearys' car, Mr. Cleary looked worried. "Look," he said, "I've had an emergency come up with a client of mine. I'm gonna have to fly down to New Orleans to sort something out."

"Are you gonna be back in time for graduation?" Misty said.

"Shouldn't be a problem," he said. "I'm just worried about David's situation." He turned to me. "What did your father say to Rothenberg's proposition?"

"He said no deal."

"No deal." Mr. Cleary took a long, slow breath. "If there's no deal, then Rothenberg'll be coming after you. I think you need to get out of town."

"Where would I go?"

"You have grandparents you could go to? A cousin, an uncle?"

I shook my head.

Mr. Cleary didn't speak for a minute. Instead Mrs. Cleary

said, "We all need to leave. Right now. David, you need to come with us."

"Where?"

Mr. and Mrs. Cleary looked at each other. "We'll drive down to Boston," Mr. Cleary said. "I know a guy in the FBI office there. We'll give them the papers, we'll explain what's going on, and everything will get sorted out."

"Can I go get my stuff?"

Mr. Cleary shook his head. "Nope. You'll have to come back for it. You can buy toothpaste and underpants in Boston."

I thought about it for a minute. There was something that was bugging me, something that had been bugging me ever since I left Leo's trailer. I just wasn't sure what it was.

"I want to check on Leo," I said.

Mr. Cleary shook his head. "He'll be fine. Rothenberg wants the papers. You've got the papers. So you're the one in danger."

"Something wasn't right," I said. "I think he needs our help. Could he come with us?"

Mr. Cleary looked at his watch.

"Look, Roger," Mrs. Cleary said to Mr. Cleary. "I know you're pressed for time. Why don't we drop you off, let you rent a car, you drive to the airport and do what you need to do. We'll pick up Leo and we'll go immediately to Boston."

Mr. Cleary thought for a minute. "*Straight* to Boston," he said. "Stay on the main roads and don't even stop for food."

"We'll be fine," Mrs. Cleary said.

"This guy's not joking around," Mr. Cleary said.

"I'm well aware, Roger," Mrs. Cleary said. "I'm well aware."

We dropped Mr. Cleary off at the only car rental place in town, then drove back through Dartington and out toward The Arsenal, stopping to turn in at the trailer park. A couple of sullen-looking Jackstaffs were sitting outside on folding chairs.

We parked and I got out of the SUV. "If I'm not back in two minutes," I said, "you guys call the police, then go on to Boston without me."

Misty and her mother exchanged glances, but didn't say anything to me.

"I'm serious," I said. "Go without me."

"I'm coming with you," Misty said.

"No you're not, young lady," Misty's mom said.

"You can't tell me what to do!" Misty said.

I could tell Misty's mom was as stubborn and strong-willed as she was. I wasn't *about* to get in the middle of that fight. I slammed the door and ran through the woods. The sun had been hot and bright back in the parking lot. But here in the woods everything was dark and quiet.

I burst out into the clearing. There was Leo's rusting

trailer. I ran up and banged on the door. "Leo!" I called. "Leo?"

There was no answer.

I banged again.

Still no answer. So I opened the door and walked in. "Leo?" I said.

Silence. Then I saw Leo. He was lying on Nolan's bed, facedown, motionless. There was something red on the pillow next to his face.

"Leo!" I shouted.

For a minute I was sure he was dead.

But then he turned toward me and said, "I'm sorry."

His face was red and purple, like somebody had punched him a couple of times.

"For what?" I said.

He gave me this weird face. "I tried to warn you, dude," he said sadly. "You should have just . . ." He sighed loudly.

And then it all fell into place. When I was in his trailer before, he had asked me if I had made copies. Why would he have cared?

"Did they have a camera on you?" I said.

He laughed sadly, then pointed to a tiny closet in the back of the trailer. "This huge dude was in there watching us the whole time. He told me to ask you if you had made copies. He said if I didn't, he'd kill me. Me and you both."

For about half a second I felt betrayed. But what else

could he have done? And he *had* tried to warn me. Blinking his eyes, telling me something in that really quiet voice. And then saying he was sorry as I left. He'd tried his best. But he'd been in a bad spot.

"And the thing about Mr. Entwhistle?" I said.

He shook his head. "They made me say it."

"Then for God's sake tell me the truth, huh? What really happened?"

There was a long pause. "You need to get out of here."

"Tell me!"

Leo sighed. "Look, truth is, Nolan went out there to meet your mom. She had called him and said, 'We need to talk.' So he went out to meet her in the Barrens. By the time he got there, she was dead. He saw one of the keys to the safe on the ground next to her. He picked it up. But in the dark I guess he couldn't see the other key. So he was never able to open the safe again."

"What about the painting? Why'd she bring it?"

Leo shrugged. "Knowing what we know now? My guess, she was going to show it to him, show him where she'd hidden the papers—that they were on the backs of paintings like that one. Maybe she was even going to give it to him."

I was going to ask him something else. But then my train of thought was interrupted. I heard footsteps outside—furtive, quiet footsteps in the grass.

Leo and I froze. For a moment it was quiet outside again.

Then another furtive footstep—this time on the other side of the trailer.

"Run!" Leo whispered.

I didn't have to be told twice.

"Here!" I said. I pulled the papers out of my pants pocket and hurled them at Leo. "Hide them." Then I yanked open the door and flew out into the yard.

But it was too late. I slammed right into the arms of the big guy that Misty had kicked in the jewels earlier. "Well, hey!" he said pleasantly. "Look what we have here."

Then he had me in a bear hug. He lifted me off the ground like I was a rag doll. I tried to struggle, but it was pointless. He must have outweighed me by a hundred and fifty pounds.

And if that wasn't bad enough, the other goon came around the other side of the trailer. He was holding some kind of wicked-looking machine gun in his hand.

"Look at the kid's face," the smaller of the two men said. "He looks like he's about to poop his drawers."

They seemed to think this was totally the funniest thing they'd ever heard. I tried to kick the big man, but it was like kicking a tree trunk. He just squeezed me tighter. I was having a hard time breathing.

"Just give us the papers, kid, and we'll be on our way."

"No!" I shouted.

He lifted me even farther up in the air and then threw me on the ground like a sack of potatoes. My head banged against the ground and everything went kind of gray and fuzzy.

I could feel the guy rummaging around in my pants, but I couldn't do anything to stop him.

After a minute, he looked up at the other guy and shook his head.

"We need to call Rothenberg," the smaller guy said.

"He's gonna tear us a new one if we don't get those papers," the bigger man said.

"Hey, so be it." The smaller of the two men pulled out a cell phone and said, "It's me, Mr. Rothenberg. Yeah, we got the kid. But no papers. Look, you need to get involved here, okay? Yeah. Yeah. At that Jackstaff kid's trailer. Right."

He hung up and then we just stood there waiting. I wondered if Misty and her mom had taken off for Boston yet. I was feeling all alone.

Then, after a couple of minutes, Mr. Rothenberg appeared at the edge of the clearing. Apparently there was a back way into the clearing. Which was good, I figured, because that meant that if Misty and her mom were still back at the parking lot, they'd be okay.

Mr. Rothenberg looked at me for a long time, then shook his head. "This has gone on way too long," he said finally.

"I'm not giving you the papers," I said. "In fact, I don't even have them anymore."

"Yeah?" he said. "Then where are they?"

"The FBI has them," I said.

He studied my face for a while. Then he said, "No, I don't think so. Try again."

"I'm not telling you."

"Shoot him in the leg," Mr. Rothenberg said to one of his goons.

The bigger of the two men pulled pointed his pistol at my leg, but didn't pull the trigger.

"No," I said firmly.

Mr. Rothenberg shook his head like he was all sad about something. "Wait a sec," he said. "Not yet, Nick." Then he yelled, "Garrett!"

Garrett walked out of the woods. In front of him was Misty. He was pointing a pistol at her back. She didn't look scared; she just looked furious.

"Look who we found sneaking through the trees with a pistol in her hand," Mr. Rothenberg said. "Unfortunately Annie Oakley here just isn't quite as big or as fast as my son."

I lay there with this horrible feeling. This was just getting worse and worse. "You should have just gone to Boston," I yelled.

Misty didn't say anything. She had little red spots on her cheeks, like she was really pissed.

"Okay, let's try again," Mr. Rothenberg said. "Where are the papers?"

"Garrett!" I yelled. "Are you out of your mind?"

Garrett had his mouth clamped shut, eyes straight ahead.

"Here's the deal," Mr. Rothenberg said. "You give up the papers, Garrett won't shoot Misty."

"Garrett!" I tried again. "Garrett, she's your *girlfriend*."

"Was," he said.

"Garrett, what's wrong with you?"

Garrett ignored me. He had his jaw set and his eyes pointed straight at Misty's back. His nose was all swollen and both of his eyes were purple from when I punched him.

"Garrett!" I called again.

"I'm not *you*, Worm," he said finally, his face dark with anger. "Just give Dad the freakin' papers."

"Where are they?" Mr. Rothenberg said.

"Okay, okay," I said. "I'll get them."

I stood up and went into Leo's trailer. Leo was sitting on the bed. The papers were lying right there next to him.

"I'm sorry," he said.

"Forget it," I said. "Anybody would have done the same thing in your position. You had no choice."

"Nolan woulda never let something like this happen," he said. "He never took crap from anybody."

"Yeah, well, that got him a couple years in jail, too, didn't it?"

"David!" Mr. Rothenberg's voice. "Hurry it up!"

I picked up the papers and walked outside.

Mr. Rothenberg strolled over and grabbed them from my hands. I felt like everything good in the world had disappeared the second they left my fingers. It was like a wave of darkness descended over my whole body.

Mr. Rothenberg snapped his fingers at one of the bodyguards. "You're a smoker, aren't you, Nick? How about a light?"

The big man pulled out a lighter, flicked it, and cupped his hands to keep the ocean breeze from putting out the light.

Mr. Rothenberg stuck the papers in the flames, let them ignite. When they were burning nicely, he tossed them up in the air. They scattered in the soft breeze, falling all around him. As they fell they caught some of the dry grass in the clearing on fire. Small tufts of flame sprouted here and there.

"See how easy that was?" Mr. Rothenberg said. "Would have been a lot better for all concerned if you'd just coughed them up in the beginning."

"What do you want us to do?" the big guy named Nick said.

"Kill 'em all," Mr. Rothenberg said. He turned and walked away. Without looking back, he said, "We'll make it look like the trailer-trash kid did it."

The two goons raised their weapons.

"I don't think so!" a voice shouted.

Mr. Rothenberg stopped but didn't turn.

I looked over at the trailer. It was Leo Jackstaff. He stood at the door, one of Nolan's old hunting rifles pointed at the Mr. Rothenberg's back.

"You shoot one of them," Leo yelled, "and I shoot you."

Mr. Rothenberg turned slowly, then sneered. "Hey, kid, I don't know if you knew it, but I went to school at The Arsenal myself. I know this place. There were Jackstaffs here when I was a kid, too. Not one of them was worth anything. I don't believe you've got the guts to do it."

"You want to know something interesting?" I said. "Jackstaffs and Crandalls come from the same family tree. And one thing about both families, they all shoot like crazy."

Mr. Rothenberg looked thoughtful. Finally he shrugged. "All right, you know what? Whatever," he said. Then he pointed his finger at me. "But remember this, kid. You got nothing. I can still help your dad. And I can still hurt him. You ever breathe a word about what happened here, you ever talk about those papers, you ever try to blame me for what happened to your father—I'll use every ounce of my strength and every dime I've got to make sure he stays in jail for the rest of his life. Witnesses can be bought. Evidence can be manufactured. A million bad things can happen."

I had nothing to say. Because I knew he was right. He was a rich guy who'd do anything to win.

"Come on, guys," Mr. Rothenberg said. "Let's go."

The last pieces of paper had turned to ash by the time they were gone. I went around stomping out the tiny fires that the papers had ignited.

I kept stomping and stomping the last one, stomping until my foot hurt.

Finally Misty came over and put her arm around my shoulder. "It's over, David," she said. "It's done."

33

There were two days before graduation. During those two days, I just sat in my dorm room and wrote in my notebook. I wrote stories about all kinds of crazy stuff. Misty came over a few times and knocked on the door. But I didn't answer.

I couldn't bring myself to leave the room. And I didn't want to be in my house. After years of living in the dorms, it felt more like somebody else's house than it did like mine. And so I didn't want to be there.

I just wrote and wrote. I guess I was trying to get some things out of my system.

Garrett had left all his stuff in the room, but he never slept there. I figured he wasn't real eager to see me. I don't know why, but sometimes I went over and read the letters Mr. Rothenberg had written to him.

I should have been angry at Garrett. But I wasn't. I just felt sorrier and sorrier for him. I mean, I've caught plenty of crap from my dad. But when I look back at it honestly,

I never felt like he was mean about it. Disappointed sometimes, sure. But he never said anything mean to me, not
once. Not even after he came to believe that I'd killed the
woman he loved more than anybody in the world. Anybody,
I guess, except me. I mean, why else would he have done
what he did, if he didn't love me?

The night before graduation, the door opened and
Garrett walked in. I was sitting there writing a story in my
notebook, listening to some tunes on my iPod. He ignored
me completely and started shoving all his stuff in a box.
When he'd gotten it all packed up, he finally spoke.

"Are you gonna say *something*?" he said finally. "You want
to punch me in the face again? Huh? Free shot. Go ahead.
Free shot."

He stood there with his arms wide, looking at me with
this weird hatred in his eyes. The swelling had gone down,
but he still had purple rings around both eyes from the time
I'd hit him before.

I just shrugged, then took one earpiece out of my ear.
"Why would I want to do that?" I said. "Once is enough."

"You can't even do it, can you?" He sneered. "You got a
little mad once, did it without thinking. But now you just
don't have the guts."

"Honestly?" I said, throwing my notebook on the bed. "I
just feel sorry for you."

He stared at me.

"I've been known to do a little snooping, too, Garrett. I read all those letters from your dad." I looked out the window. I could see his father's limousine parked down at the curb. "Truth is, I feel sorry for you."

He licked his lips, kept staring at me. "That's because you're a loser," he said finally.

"I think there's a good Garrett in there," I said, "a good Garrett in there fighting to come out. You don't want to be like your dad."

"A couple of guys will come in later, take care of the boxes," he said. "There better not be anything missing."

"Whatever."

I put the earpiece back into my ear and turned up my iPod. Garrett just kept standing there.

"What?" I said finally.

He looked at me for a minute.

"What!" I said again.

"I cheated, you know," he said finally.

I made a face, showing I was irritated. "Huh?"

"First Shot," he said. "I got a lot better at shooting this year. A *lot* better. But I was never as good as you or Misty. Never even close."

"I knew that," I said. I mean, I did and I didn't. Ten tens? Something about it had always been suspect. But really, who even cared? In the grand scheme of things, it was just a dumb little game. I wasn't even sure now why I'd ever cared. There were more important things in life than blowing holes in a piece of paper.

"Don't you want to know how I did it?" he said.

There were a million ways you could cheat. Pay some guy with a scoped rifle to sit up in the Barrens and shoot off a bench rest. They could chew up the ten ring all day, never miss once. It'd be easy. But the truth was, I didn't care how he'd done it.

I picked up my notebook, looked at it, and threw it back on the bed. I was finally tired of writing. Maybe I was just bored, or maybe I'd gotten everything out of my system for now.

I cranked up my iPod, closed my eyes, and smiled. I knew it'd bug the hell out of him that he couldn't tell me how he cheated. He'd want to rub my face in it—all the details of his little plan. But, like I say, there are a million ways to cheat. Any moron can cheat. It's playing fair that takes ingenuity.

I kept my eyes closed for a long time. I may have even drifted off to sleep for a while.

When I opened them again, not only was Garrett gone, so were his boxes.

And so was the notebook I'd been writing in. For a minute I felt really pissed off. But then I got over it. There was something kind of flattering about it, that he'd actually find my stories interesting enough to be worth stealing.

34

Graduation was the next day at one o'clock. It was a beautiful day. You could see a line of dark clouds way out over the ocean's horizon, but the sky above us was blue and clear.

The stage was set up in the middle of the soccer field. All of the faculty were lined up in their academic robes on the left side of the stage. On the right were the honored guests and the people participating in the program—the valedictorian, the speaker, the minister who was giving the benediction, the board of directors, all those kind of people. I noticed Mr. Rothenberg up there with his usual smug expression on his face. Garrett sat beside him, holding his rifle. He was staring straight ahead like he was really concentrating, getting ready to make his big shot.

Seating for the seniors was alphabetical. Since Misty and I both have names that start with C, we ended up sitting next to each other. I had a feeling of apprehension—not because I was nervous about graduating—but because I had put something else in motion and wasn't sure how it would all work out.

The graduation went off like all graduations—totally boring.

The speaker was an Arsenal alumnus who was now the head of some big company that made automobile parts. He said a bunch of clichés about rigor and discipline and hard work and fairness and Winners and Achievers and blah-blah-blah, as he read a speech that had almost certainly been written by somebody in the public relations department of his company. Then the valedictorian, a guy with the really unfortunate name of Faye Cunningham IV, gave a really boring speech about rigor and discipline and hard work and fairness and Winners and Achievers and blah-blah-blah. Then Mr. Entwhistle handed out the diplomas.

Then it was time for the culmination of the program, the First Shot.

The concert band played the school anthem and then Garrett Rothenberg stood up and marched to the front of the stage carrying his rifle. He wore the school uniform from a hundred and fifty years ago. Gray, with silver buttons and epaulets and dark blue stripes down the seams. The shadow from the tall blue hat didn't quite hide the shiners. As soon as the anthem was over, everybody in the concert band sat down except for one of the drummers. He began a long slow drumroll.

Garrett looked nervous. He lifted his rifle. I found myself

holding my breath. At the far end of the stage, the target was raised on a pole. It was a simple iron circle about the size of a human heart, painted red. An easy shot from fifty yards. But still, it was an unbroken tradition, two hundred and eleven years or whatever it was. A lot of pressure. I wanted him to make his shot.

Once Garrett had raised his rifle and aimed it at the target, the drummer ceased. All you could hear was the distant thump of waves on the beach, the cry of seabirds, the fluttering of cloth in the soft wind off the ocean. The crowd was completely silent.

For a moment Garrett's hands shook violently.

He's gonna miss! I thought. *He's gonna freakin' miss!*

But then his hands steadied. *There you go. Steady now. It's all in the breathing.*

The crowd waited. A muscle tensed in his hand, and his finger began to tighten. For half a second, there was a strange lull, as though the entire earth had paused to listen. No waves crashing, no gulls crying, no wind.

Then a tiny sound. A dry snap, like the breaking of a twig.

For a moment, Garrett didn't move.

"What happened?" the kid sitting to my left said.

"It's a hang fire," Misty said from my right. "He pulled the trigger, but his gun didn't go off."

Garrett lowered the rifle a few inches, then turned slightly, an odd smile on his face.

"What is he *doing*?" Misty said. "He should be pointing it up in the air!"

"He's got that fancy rifle," I said. "It never hangs fire. I guess he's not used to it doing that."

Then there was a loud bang and a puff of smoke.

Then someone behind me said, "Oh my God!"

35

They rushed Mr. Rothenberg to the hospital, but there was nothing that could be done. Shot right in the heart, same as my mom. The bizarre accident made the news in Boston and in all the stations in Maine. But it never went national. It was a sad and ironic fluke, the gun going off just when it happened to be pointed right at Garrett's own father's heart. *The Boston Globe* ran an editorial about how bad guns were, how "antediluvian traditions," which put weapons in the hands of "children," practically guaranteed that people would be shot.

The board of directors immediately convened and voted to end the practice of First Shot entirely, and to disband the Dartington Rifles. It was "a tradition whose time had long passed," the acting chairman of the board said.

And that was the end of it.

Well . . . almost.

• • •

The day after graduation, three very highly paid lawyers retained by the firm of Rothenberg, Lyttle & Company flew up from New York City and had a long conference with the district attorney of Devonshire County.

An hour later, the state of Maine let my father go. The district attorney of Devonshire County released a statement about how a "tragic chain of miscommunications" had resulted in the arrest of the wrong man. A witness had come forward who had proved to the satisfaction of local law enforcement that the murder had been committed by another man—a man who had since died—with the result that no prosecution was possible.

The day Dad got released from jail, he and Misty and I took a tour of The Arsenal together. Dad had handed in his resignation that morning. He said it would be best for the institution if he moved on. Besides, he said, he was ready for a change.

We walked slowly through Crandall House, looking at all the old paintings of the Crandalls. They were tough, hard-looking men. Behind all the fancy clothes and the powdered wigs and stuff, they still looked like guys you wouldn't really want to mess with.

"So what are you going to do now, Mr. Crandall?" Misty said.

"I think I'm going to try doing some writing again," Dad said.

"David said you used to be a writer," Misty said. "Why'd you stop?"

Dad looked thoughtful. "I guess I could say that circumstances intervened. But that's really just an excuse. The truth is, I just was never sure that you could make a difference as a writer. Here, you're affecting people's lives, changing the way young men and women see the world forever. You write a book or a story?" He shrugged. "Who knows if it ever makes a difference."

"What do you think, David?" Misty said.

"Oh, I *know* a story can affect people's lives," I said.

"You sound awful sure of that," Dad said. I noticed that he'd been looking at me differently since he got out of jail. Like he was really proud of me.

"I am," I said.

I thought about this story I had written the other day. It was called "Hang Fire," a story about this prince back in the good ol' days, who rigs up his hunting gun so that it'll go off at the wrong time. Then he kills his evil father accidentally on purpose and releases himself from a terrible, ancient spell. Kind of a hokey, fantasy-type story. Not my usual thing. But parts of it were totally real. For instance, it had a very technical explanation for how you'd alter the weapon to make it hang fire for exactly five seconds.

But what's the big picture? If a story works, if it touches another person's life—who can say there's anything wrong with it? Poor old Garrett. He was looking for something—

anything—that would get him out of the rattrap of a life he'd found himself living. My story just spelled it all out, showed him a precise and clear way to eliminate the source of his misery.

Did I leave that notebook sitting there on my bed intentionally? Did I expect him to steal it? And if so, did I think he'd actually carry through with the plan laid out in the story?

Not really. It was just one of those things. I mean, I was sitting there looking at Garrett, and this thought just flitted across my mind. *What if?* You know? *What if?* Like an experiment.

And what's the lesson from the experiment? The lesson is, if you dream something, it might just happen. For good or ill.

That's what First Shot is all about. The thing they're trying to teach us at The Arsenal is this: *Ideas have consequences.* When you're a kid, most of the time you think of something and it just sits there in your head, an empty little thought. *Someday I'm gonna be a pro ballplayer! Someday I'm gonna be president!* After a while, the thought floats off and you have another thought. *Someday I'm gonna go the moon.* Big whoop.

But at a certain point in life, it's not like that anymore. At a certain point, you have a thought, and the thought flies off and something happens. Something real. Like a bullet flying out of a gun. And that thing that happens—what*ever* it is—you own it. Good or bad, it's yours.

So. Do I feel guilty that in some small way I pointed Garrett toward the terrible thing he did? Not really. It's his life. It's not like I put a gun to *his* head. He had a choice and he made it. Sure, I feel a little queasy and weird about it. I wrote some dumb little fantasy in a story. And then it turned into reality. Okay. Fine. Here's the thing. What happened, it's justice. Mr. Rothenberg deserved what happened to him. He hired a guy to kill my mom because she wanted to expose him for stealing all that money. Garrett told this to the district attorney.

And Garrett? Maybe Garrett will be a better person now that his dad's out of the picture. I hope so. I mean, clearly the guy's got a screw loose. But things *do* change. I know I'm a lot happier than I was nine months ago. Do I still feel sad about Mom? Sure. I'll never get over that completely. But at least now it's a settled thing. There's some comfort in knowing what happened, and in seeing the guilty get punished. I'm ready to move on, go to college, move on to whatever's next. I'm tired of looking backward, back toward the past.

"Let's get outta here," I said.

We walked slowly out of Crandall Hall, the old hard-eyed Crandalls looking down at us, neither judging us, nor approving. And for a minute, I felt like I was one of them.

So, I don't know, maybe I'm not an appendix after all. Maybe the Great Crandalls are about to stage a comeback.